STORM SWIFT
MISSING IN ACTION

The exciting, action packed adventure sequel
to Storm Swift and the Seventh Key

Stephanie de Winter

Amazon Publishing

Cover design by: Heather Innes
Illustrations: Oliver Bland
Library of Congress Control Number: 2018675309
Printed in the United States of America

*To my children Tara Rose & Krystian and to
my mother Kathleen Rose with love.*

Be yourself; everyone else is already taken.

Always allow your inner light to shine. Do not let anyone dim your brilliance...

OSCAR WILDE & STEPHANIE DE WINTER

CONTENTS

PREFACE

Finn awoke. He was lying on cold concrete in complete darkness. The smell of oil mixed with sea salt wafted around him. Machinery hummed nearby. He was inside some kind of building. Trying to accustom his eyes to the dark, shapes slowly began to form. Shady images. A crack of light like an upside down 'L' must be a door. A locked door has hinges. The hinges were the weakest point. If he could free himself from his restraints, he'd have a chance. His hands were taped behind his back and his legs, knees and feet had also been tied together.

CHAPTER 1
A Storm is Brewing

Storm sat at the dining room table, chewing the end of her pencil. Rock music blasted through her headphones, pulsating, and circling her brain. Her drawing of a small puffin, sitting on a grey and yellow speckled rock, was lopsided with a disproportionate orange beak. The art project set by Grandad Flint, involved drawing a variety of seabirds. However, Storm was struggling with the task. Her brain knew how a puffin should appear on paper, but her hand didn't seem able to coordinate this. It was clear to Storm, that she hadn't inherited her mother's talent for drawing or painting. Her mother, Lily Swift, was making a name for herself, as a talented artist. Her paintings were dramatic, full of energy and were currently being exhibited in art galleries in Edinburgh and London.

Finn Locke, Storm's fifteen-year-old cousin, sat sprawled in the chair opposite her, adding finishing touches to his drawing. His puffin, in contrast, was lifelike and faultless. Storm half expected it to open its' beak, squawk and fly off, out over the dark ocean. Pulling out her air pods, she observed the intense concentration on his face.

"That's so good Finn." She smiled. "You have a real talent."

He glanced at it critically. His dark blue eyes full of scorn.

"So. So." He smiled, noting her attempt. "Can't have it all Storm."

Storm threw her pencil at him.

"And stop kicking me with your great, giant feet!"

Finn grinned. He was tall and broad for his age, standing at over six feet tall. His long legs took up most of the space under the dining room table. He stood up, stretched, and added logs to the log burner. The fire crackled and hissed greedily, devouring the rotting morsels. The picture window showed a stormy dark bay. Patches of yellow brilliance battled through the thick grey cloud, casting patches of light upon the water. Fife sat in the distance under a vast black cloud.

The September air was brisk. A northerly wind chill plummeting temperature on Puffin Island, home to Storm, Finn, and their family. The Island was a nature haven, situated amid the Firth of Forth estuary, on the east coast of Scotland. It had been in the family for generations.

Lily Swift, Storm's Mother and Finn's aunt, poked her head around the door.

"Grandad Flint and I are off to Edinburgh." She placed a kit list on the table. "You'll need to start packing. The weekend will be here before you know it!"

"Ok!" snapped Storm, her olive eyes glaring into her mothers.

Finn glanced at Storm sharply before smiling at Aunt Lily.

"We'll make sure we start it today Aunt Lily."

Lily, stared anxiously at Storm and sighed. Her daughter's face was hidden by tresses of dark emerald green hair, as she bent studiously over the drawing, attempting to resize the puffin's beak.

After making an appointment at the hairdressers to restore her green hair back to blonde, Storm changed her mind about the colour at the last minute. The dark emerald green had faded to an insipid shade of lime green, and something needed to be done; but, as she sat in the hairdresser's black leather chair, she realised that she preferred the 'Storm' she had become, since colouring it dark emerald. The action of dying her hair, had triggered a series of events, subsequently freeing her from the stress of attending hell school and granting her the relief of home school with a chance to progress in life. Storm's anxiety levels had decreased considerably since being taught at home and she felt stronger and more in control of her life and emotional wellbeing. The emerald green hair was here to stay.

Lily walked over and stroked her daughter's hair soothingly.

"You'll enjoy it. It'll be good for you to mix with other people your age."

Storm grimaced. It had been three months since home schooling had begun, and she'd adapted well, making a massive effort to complete the work set. Finn had also chosen to be taught from home rather than return to Shelley High School, and time had accelerated, packed full of laughter, learning and enjoyment.

Now her mother had decided to ruin all the progress made, by sending them to an autumn adventure camp, to mix with other young people. Prior to this announcement, Storm's anxiety levels had decreased considerably, as they seemed to be provoked by a demand such as school attendance or an activity that included staying overnight somewhere.

Grandad Flint appeared and ruffled her hair.

"It's only a week Storm!"

The family simply didn't understand. They thought she would lack the social skills needed to function in society if she didn't put herself in social situations. However, she and Finn regularly went over to the mainland to meet friends, and so it wasn't as if they were completely cut off. Considering her past, riddled with school anxiety, Storm felt she was now quite sociable and making considerable improvement. But now this!

Dread and fear uncurled from its place of rest, stretching, and flexing its muscles. Anxiety having been dormant for some time was raring to go and ready to leap into action!

After her mother and Grandad Flint left the room. Storm sat with her head in her hands.

"You go Finn. You like that sort of thing. I just can't. I feel sick!"

"I'll be there, Storm. Can help if you feel weird…"

"You don't get it Finn!" Storm shouted. "I can't sleep anywhere I don't know! Sharing a room with other girls is my idea of hell! Literally a living nightmare!"

"That's why Aunt Lily thinks…"

"I'm not ready Finn!" Storm stood up scraping back her chair. "I can literally feel demons waking up in my head at the thought of it!"

"Let's go for a swim or walk or something." Finn shut the door of the log burner. "You're like nearly fifteen and I think they think you need this."

"THEY don't know what it's like! Just pretending to be all nice and get it! Otherwise, they wouldn't be ruining everything! Just when…just when I'm…" Storm started crying tears of frustration.

"Hey Storm. Come on." Finn said sympathetically. "We'll sort something out."

"When I'm ready to go to camp I'll say! It will just happen. When I'm ready I will be!" Storm yelled. "Forcing it? No! It's gonna bring my anxiety back. I can't do that again. I'd rather die!"

Finn shook his head.

"That's mental talk!" Finn looked worried. "I get it. Course I do."

"Nobody does!" Storm screamed at him, shredding the kit list, before casting the paper fragments up into the air.

The offensive paper floated like snowflakes gently down onto the shiny mahogany surface of the dining table. Grabbing her thick black hoody Storm left the Light House, slamming the front door violently behind her. Her mood was as dark as the elements and unwelcome tears mingled with rainwater and sea spray flowing down her cheeks. Storm headed off through the small forest towards the west beach.

Back in March her life had been hell. Full of torment. School anxiety had spiralled out of control and in desperation she had dyed her hair dark green to be suspended from Shelley Hell School, in the hope that she could prove that home schooling was a more suitable option. Her family agreed to try home schooling, and her cousin Finn had come to stay on Puffin Island with his mother Molly. For the first time in years her life had been full of laughter, happiness, and peace.

But now an earthquake threatened to shatter and destroy her fragile world. Her mum and Grandad Flint simply didn't understand how carefully balanced her mental health was. She was learning and developing resilience daily, especially how to cope with stressful situations. But it was a gradual process. It was cruel and unhealthy to plunge her into an environment that she simple wasn't ready for.

Finn's deep voice rumbled, carrying on the wind as he ran to catch her up. At six foot two Finn had long legs and was physically in good shape. His dark olive skin, in contrast to her pale complexion, made her feel like a cold creature, or the living dead, next to his glowing vitality.

"Jez cuz. Calm your beans!" He grabbed her arm.

"Was happy and felt…I've never felt happy like this before. And now this!" Storm shook her head in despair.

"Maybe say. Tell them. If it's causing this much shit for you Storm." Finn said seriously.

"Tried. Last night." Storm pressed her palms to her forehead looking out across the writhing sea. "It's cos Mum's got this exhibition in Edinburgh. Then she's heading up to Shetland to meet Dad for the weekend. And Grandad Flints off to some Veteran thing. So I've got to have my whole life ruined!"

"Dramatico!" Finn tried to make light of her outburst.

Storm glared at him and ran along to the cliff top and scrambling down the sandy slop to the beach. Months before they had lain at this very spot on the top of the cliff, secretly watching trespassers come aboard the island, loaded with bags full of counterfeit money. The gang had ventured into the Cave of Boulders, situated at the end of the beach, to store their stash, for pick up. But later that night, their small boat was smashed to smithereens on the rocks during a violent storm. It seemed like a long time ago, now to Storm. Running to the cave, she hurled smaller boulders from the entrance and clambered into the cave. Finn scrambled in after her.

Storm and Finn now used the cave as a retreat. It was sheltered from the elements, and rocks were piled up at the entrance. It was a haven and an excellent hiding place. They'd rearranged the boulders and made a small fireplace to add heat and light. Finn kept the pile of firewood topped up regularly. He removed a large boulder that covered the man-made chimneystack. Kindling, candles and brittle firewood were stacked at the back of the cave. Finn prepared a small fire and lit it. A thin spiral of smoke headed out of the chimney, filling the small space with warmth and cheer.

Storm placed her hand just above her stomach.

"Feel all uncomfortable again." Her stomach growled in agreement.

Finn put his arm around her. They sat in the cave side by side.

"I don't mind going; but we could think of a way for you not to go." He said. "Gonna look suspicious if we both don't go. Mum's heading back to that retreat place in Mull for two weeks, leaving today, so the Island will be empty."

"Hippy Clare's house sitting! Why can't they just leave us here?"

"They think a week's too long." Finn said. "Apparently we're too young."

"Well I'm not going!" Storm said stubbornly. "I'll go live in the Locked Room chamber. Have access to the Boat House Cabin for a bathroom. Be safe down there."

"Spend a week on your own?" Finn frowned. "What if something happened?"

"Got my phone." Storm sighed. "I'll wait until Mum's out and email the place."

"It's called Tyne Adventures, Mum sent me the details of the week's booking and activities. You might go nuts, a week on your own!"

"Go nuts if I go. From the stress! I just can't cope with it yet Finn." Storm looked down at her hands morosely.

"I know." Finn squeezed her. "What's the plan?"

"What you don't know...and all that. I'll think of something."

CHAPTER 2
The Fraudulent Email

Returning to the Light House, Finn cooked fried eggs on toast, washed down with steaming hot chocolate.

"My culinary masterpiece." He declared bringing the food up from the kitchen into the warm dining room.

Storm sat on the window seat in black hoody and track trousers, staring out to sea. She seemed deflated and defeated as if the life force had drained from her body.

"You made it?" She asked, turning in surprise.

"Yes. I made it. Be on Master Chef this time next year." Finn announced proudly.

Storm smiled weakly. Uncurling she walked over to the table.

"We're here for each other yeah!" Finn said. "Let's make a plan and stick to it. Course I'll help. I always have your back. You know that."

Storm nodded.

"Thanks Finn." Storm chucked a log on the hissing fire and purple and orange flames curled around it licking the wood. Sitting down she took a sip of the sweet chocolate. "Means a lot."

"So cheer up you miserable bee..arch!" Finn grinned pretending to duck.

Storm grinned taking a mouthful of egg and toast.

"That's not bad. No snotty egg and seasoned. Impressto!"

"Welcome back! Storm has returned! You can be one scary wee dude!" Finn declared. "Problems need solutions. End of. We'll find one." His brow creased in thought.

Storm waited until her mother left the art studio to take a bath. Lily loved baths, and always spent at least half an hour soaking in hot lemon scented water. Relaxing classical music for bath time, tinkled in the distance. Candles were lit. The bathroom door clicked shut.

Creeping like a cat burglar, Storm sneaked into her mother's studio. The room was full of easels, and finished paintings. There was one left to complete. Lily had been working hard. The Studio boasted a vast picture window looking out over the ocean, and the roof consisted of glass. The light was perfect for painting. The room smelt of paint. Speeding over to the table in the corner, Storm opened her mother's laptop. It asked for an access password. Storm typed in: Storm2005. The password page opened to 'desktop'. Clicking on the puffin email icon, Storm scanned the email list for the confirmation email from Tyne Adventures. Composing a new email, she frantically typed in their email address. Pausing for a second, she added the content:

"Good evening. Unfortunately, due to personal circumstances, Storm Swift will be unable to attend the adventure week in October. She may attend adventure camp another time, so don't worry about refunding the payment, as I will contact you at a later date about this. Please note that I have changed my email address to LilySSwift@pmail.com so please can you reply on this email in future. I have also changed my mobile number to: 77941098777. This is now my contact number. Finn Locke will still be attending and should this change, I will let you know.

Kind regards Lily Swift."

Storm took a deep breath. She'd created a new email account and given her own mobile number to cover her tracks. Her fraudulent activities left her feeling queasy, but the thought of attending the autumn camp was a worse feeling of dread. Pressing the send button, the dishonest act was complete. Hovering nervously, she awaited the possible acknowledgement email. It pinged to the 'in- box'. Storm immediately deleted it. Clicking on the sent folder, she deleted her email to Tyne Adventures and the two messages from the trash. Shaking with nervous treachery, Storm shut down the laptop and fled to the warmth of the Zen room, up in the lighthouse tower. Finn was still using the Zen room viewing platform as a bedroom, while the outhouses were being converted into living accommodation for his mother, and himself.

The Zen room walls were made of reinforced glass from floor to ceiling. Situated four meters below the lighthouse lamp, the views across Fife, Edinburgh and East Lothian were spectacular. Cream comfy sofas, a small wood burner and beanbags slouched there. Storm was fortunate to have the tower as her own accommodation, separate from Grandad Flint and her mother. A spiral staircase ran up the height of the lighthouse that housed the Lamp at the very top that was now automated. The Zen room sat below, and directly beneath, was Storms' bedroom, and five steps below that, her bathroom.

The lighthouse tower was attached to the rest of the house, named the Light House. The Light House had been renovated years before and extended. It had many levels due to being built originally on a volcanic hill. Beneath the two cellars lay an underground world that Storm and Finn had discovered months earlier. Hidden below was a secret passageway, Emerald Pool Chamber, Creepy Cave and a Ghost Ship. There were also three storage rooms, one hidden behind a Locked Door that hid secrets from shipwrecks, that could only be imagined. But for them it was a reality they had discovered.

"The deed is done." Storm sat next to Finn on the floor next to the fire. She was shaking with adrenalin.

Finn nodded.

"Still not sure it's the best idea...but...no! Don't go mental again, Storm. I get it. Just you on your own all week. Can't see how they won't find out, at some point."

"It's radio silence." Storm said heatedly. "The camp rules. No phone calls whilst we're there at Tyne Adventures, unless it's obviously an emergency. So how can they?"

"They'll see us onto the train. How will you get back?"

"I'll manage. Get off at the first stop, and head back to the Boat House Cabin, then down into the tunnel. Probably sleep in the Locked Room."

"Creepy!"

Storm shook her head.

"Nah. It's home. I know every inch of it down there. Plus, if I get creeped out I can sneak to my bedroom. Hippy Clare will probably be stoned on weed and pass out!"

"And they say your mental health's tragic! What about hers? "

"Exactly. They leave a weed head to guard Puffin Island! We don't do alcohol or drugs; and yet, we have to be shipped out."

Finn shook his head.

"Totally. Wish I wasn't going now. Would rather stay here. We could go diving and explore the Firth of Forth for shipwrecks and treasure. We have wet suits and all the gear."

"I wish you weren't too. I hope they don't email Aunt Molly

saying sorry Mum's cancelled my booking."

"If they do she won't get it until she's finished her two weeks on Mull as she has no internet there. Something to do with them not being allowed, as could hamper recovery. Plus, I think Aunt Lily took care of the booking."

"Oh what a tangled web we weave!" Storm declared dramatically. "I feel bad."

"You should." He looked at her quizzically. "What tangled web you on about?"

"Jez you're ignorant! It's Sir Walter Scott."

"Who?"

"Oh my God. The Walter Scott Monument by Waverly Station! Edinburgh! You have heard of Edinburgh!"

"Err yeah 'course!"

"He's like a major Scottish poet, writer...You dumb ass!"

Finn battered her with a cushion.

"Ow." Storm laughed. "'Oh, what a tangled web we weave, when first we practice to deceive'. Basically, bullshit is complex, and more and more lies are told to cover up the first lie, until it's a total chaotic mess."

"Oh right. Makes sense. See home schools paying off."

"For me, but Finn you took the same class." She laughed at his blank expression. "Sure your heads not still full of water from that storm you nearly drowned in?"

Finn laughed.

"Prob had a fish swim in my ear and nibbling my brain."

"Ew."

They burst out laughing.

"Let's get up early tomorrow and go swimming in the Emerald

Pool Chamber and explore the Creepy Cave and Ghost Ship."

"Can take a packed breakfast and lunch as we have no lessons. Grandad Flint has some meeting he has to attend on the mainland."

"Excellent idea." Finn scratched his head. "You trust me yeah?"

"Course. With my actual life."

"Same. As in vice versa. I'm gonna give you some money....no don't interrupt. I'll be worried sick otherwise. So, it's kinda for me as well as helping you. That wad of cash, my dad left me in the Locked Room. I'll give you some of that. Leave part of it in the Cave of Boulders, bit in the Locked Room, and the rest you take with you. We know, from experience that things seldom go to plan. Peace of mind Storm. Please?"

Storm nodded.

"Since you put it like that. I'll pay you back."

Finn looked worried.

"Just don't have the best feeling Storm."

"Prob anxiety about the camp."

"Hmm...maybe. Don't suffer from anxiety though Storm. Have this weird ache in my stomach."

"Maybe from your cooking?" Storm joked innocently, trying to lighten the atmosphere.

Finn smiled; but his dark eyes full of concern, bored into hers. He did not feel happy about the situation. His intuition was usually correct. Earlier that year, he'd experienced an overwhelming feeling regarding his father, who was missing in action, from Special Forces. Convinced, he was hiding out in the Locked Room in the secret passageway, he'd even tried picking the lock. He'd known, without actually knowing, that his dad, Josh, was hidden behind the 'Locked Door', alive and not dead, like many others had thought, and tried to convince him. And he'd been right. His dad had indeed been hidden there, as part of an undercover operation to smash a gang of organised criminals, dealing in counterfeit money.

However, the intuition, he was experiencing right now, held an additional element. Fear! Gripping, cold dread twisted inside his guts. But was the uncomfortable feeling connected to Storm's plan to stay on her own for a week beneath Puffin Island, or was it connected to heading off to adventure camp alone? One thing was for certain, for the first time in his life, Finn sincerely hoped that his intuition was wrong. Because if it was not. One of them or both of them, were heading for danger, possibly peril!

CHAPTER 3
The Underworld of Puffin Island

Finn's alarm buzzed at six am. Dressing hastily, he ran down the spiral staircase to Storm's bedroom below, rapping on her door.

"I'm ready." Storm emerged and they moved quietly to the kitchen.

Finn filled a flask with hot vegetable soup, and another with steaming hot chocolate while Storm packed cheese and onion pasties, chicken and ham sandwiches, crisps, grapes, and chocolate into her black rucksack. Armed with torches, they headed down to the lower cellar. Taking the keys from behind the old painting of Puffin Island named: 'Keeper of Keys' they removed the potato sacks, revealing a wooden trapdoor; the entrance to the underworld below.

Taking one of the smaller keys, Storm clicked open the top lock, followed by the two side locks and finally, the bottom lock of the trapdoor. Swinging back the door onto the cellar flagstone, she removed the thin wood covering that disguised the entrance as a mere storage space. Inserting the larger key into the slab's brass keyhole, Storm slid the mechanism down and back, revealing a deep black hole. Clambering down the iron rungs she disappeared into the passage below, Finn followed, closing the trap door behind him.

A familiar blast of cold air, mustiness and sea salt assailed their senses, as they made their way along the winding passageway, passing the alcove to the right that led to the Emerald Pool Chamber. Storm smiled at the sight of the Locked Door further to the left. She called to Finn. The beam of torchlight bobbed along the dark ancient door.

"This nearly drove us nuts!" she chuckled, referring to the Locked Door.

Finn laughed.

"I know. Trying to find the Key to the Locked Door was like impossible." he shook his head. "But we cracked it!"

"With the help of Dad's old schoolbook: 'Treasure Island'. This place is the keeper of secrets for sure," agreed Storm.

"Defo is. Need to make sure you have everything for Friday. Are you still set on staying?" He glanced at Storm in the hope that by some miracle she'd changed her mind.

Storm nodded.

"Yep. I am. The storage rooms are packed with supplies Finn, so I won't starve. But I'll bring my own and just use those in an emergency."

"Just wish I could get rid of this anxiety." Finn grumbled, rubbing the area of his solar plexus situated in the area above his stomach. "It's a feeling like something bad's gonna happen. Like a kinda dread."

"You're such a cave man." Storm laughed.

"I actually really am." He flexed his biceps. "Me cave man!" His muscles bulged.

"Like oh wow! Look at the size of them!"

"Been working out daily. And running. You should try it."

Storm nodded.

"Been doing some yoga and toning and just started running, but still slow."

"It'll come. Healthy body. Healthy mind. It's just practise and repetition."

They reached the storage room to the right that housed the diving equipment and a rack of linen and towels.

"Jenny was supposed to be coming round tomorrow. Questions will be asked about camp and other stuff…"

"Maybe say things are too hectic with camp coming up. See her when you get back." Finn suggested. "Things are complicated enough without involving best mates."

"Truth. You like Jenny alright?" Storm checked a small air cylinder and picked up the wet suit.

"I do. She's like genuine." Finn nodded.

"She likes you. We wearing these? Think I will."

"Course she does. Who could possibly resist!" Finn laughed. "Yeah, let's put them on as it's not so warm. You might freeze to death down here!"

"I'll be fine. So, Jenny?"

Finn stood with his hands on his hips and burst out laughing.

"She's asked you yeah? To see if I like her."

"I told her I'd be rubbish at it. We're too close you and I. Said you'd see right through."

"Is like super obvious cuz!" Finn changed into his wet suit. "Dunno to be honest. She's a bit young, and your mate, and a bit fussy."

"Fussy?"

"Bit motherly which is kinda weird at fourteen."

"Err maybe she just gives a shit about people!"

"Dunno yet anyway."

"About her?"

"What is this?" Finn chucked a belt at Storm to attach her air cylinder to. They were using small oxygen tanks that contained air up to ninety minutes. "You practising interrogation? Gonna get a job in Special Forces like your old man?"

"And your old man. Maybe. Good deflection!"

"What?"

"Change of subject. Oh, forget it. Forget I mentioned it."

"Are you thinking of a career in the military?" Finn quizzed.

"Maybe. Been watching lots of stuff on the internet about the training and stuff."

"Thought we were gonna be intrepid explorers and treasure seekers? Locke and Swift!"

"Or Swift and Locke. Could do both. Just been thinking about what to do in the future. Be a bit painful for you but maybe try it!" Storm ran off at speed, laughing, towards the Emerald Pool Chamber.

Finn raced after her, grinning. Laden down with the equipment and bags, he panted with exertion.

"Leave me to lug it all Storm!" He yelled.

His loud voice bounced off the stone walls, echoing throughout the passageways.

Storm's laughter tinkled back at him.

Lifting the slab to the entrance of the chamber, Storm and Finn, made their way down the slate steps to the small tunnel that led to the sealed door of the Emerald Pool Chamber. Storm unlocked it with the fifth key. There was a loud clunk. Moving about the chamber, they lit the numerous lanterns and candles seated on the natural shelf that ran around the cavern. Firelight flickered and the green water of the lagoon, gleamed invitingly.

Crouching, Finn felt the water.

"Ooh now that is cold! Not had it heated yet then! Tut tut and with all that wealth!"

Storm laughed.

"Yeah, as you said. The family might put electricity and heating down here. Especially with all the hidden riches!"

"Maybe for the future." Said Finn. "But there is light in the room beyond the Locked Door."

"Yeah. I may camp out in there. It's like super safe."

Finn nodded with approval.

"Let's have a drink then head out."

Placing a blanket on the cold wide rocky ledge at the head of the pool, they sat upon its cosy warmth. Finn poured hot chocolate out into mugs. A warm vapour rose like puffs of smoke into the cold air. The smell of chocolate filled their nostrils. Finn's stomach growled with hunger and Storm handed him a cheese and onion pasty, biting into one herself.

"Wow, I'm like a cookery genius." Storm nodded her head approvingly, winding her long dark green hair up into a bun on the top of her head. "I might become, like a world-famous cook instead of an intrepid explorer, or Captain in Special Forces."

"You did not make them!" Finn's eyes gleamed with pleasure, as he munched enthusiastically. He took another from the pile. "They are like so good!"

"I did. I told you I cook when I've got anxiety. Pretty much filled up the freezer last week, with all the talk of adventure camp."

"Defo have to make you anxious more Storm. Sneak into your room at night and tell you over and over you have to return to Shelley High School."

Storm glared at him.

"Too soon?"

"Yeah, too soon and that's just creepy!"

Finn laughed a deep throaty infectious sound. Storm joined in.

"You're such a weirdo." She punched him fondly on the arm.

"But you love it." He burst out laughing. "Like ow!"

"Jenny?" Storm's eyes gleamed with merriment.

"You don't give up. Nah not interested at the mo Storm. Just moved here, to the island, and loving it. Got all this." Finn gestured to the Emerald Pool Chamber. "Getting over the situ with John the Psycho and Mum. Just been a lot. Plus, I'm too young for all that."

"So, when you said 'dunno yet anyway?' It's what you meant?"

Finn looked down and then at Storm.

"It's complicated. I'm like a bit older than you , and it does make a bit of difference." He drained his hot chocolate. "Don't want to talk about it right now, but yeah another time. Just don't judge me."

"I never would and you're like nine months older."

Dressed in wet suits with air cylinders and underwater torches, they submerged into the pool, and swam the length leading to the Archway and the entrance to the Creepy Cave. A wisp of green seaweed waved, beckoning them in. Swimming through the arch they passed the Dome of Breath 1, a dome shaped air pocket, and swam down the murky tunnel. The boulder that had fallen, partially blocking the entrance to the Creepy Cave, was still there and they squeezed past it out into the waters of the adjoining cavern.

Strange brown, orange and green plants grew amidst the limpet encrusted speckled rocks and boulders. They swam upwards through the gloom. The sudden dark desolate shape of the Ghost Ship emerged, eerily looming out of the fog, with its sinister coral eye sockets that had once been proud gleaming brass port holes viewing the adventures of the world.

Swimming down the starboard side, then upwards to where the ship's bridge had been, they swam past the captain's once splendid cabin, now full of rotten wood and rubble. This was where Storm had discovered her first piece of treasure. An ancient silver candle holder.

They swam through the icy blanket of silent darkness, plunging deeper into the terrifying obscurity of the unknown. Fear was welcome, as it brought with it, an alertness needed while exploring the abandoned, underwater tomb. Storm led the way through rooms full of tinder, sand, and shells, with the odd bunk that was still intact. What had happened to the sailors that night? Storm wondered. They had yet to discover human remains. A skull or bones. Had there been a battle or a violent storm that had caused the wreckage? Had the crew died or survived the trauma that the Ghost Ship endured that fateful night? Questions hammered at her mind as she swam. Finn and Storm stopped at a shape resembling a table. It was now encrusted with sea anemone. On the rough surface was a long lump of coral. Finn added it to the small sack on his belt.

Tapping his watch Finn pointed upwards. Turning, they hurriedly paddled upwards, breaking the surface of water.

"Let's go through the coded archway and then have lunch." Storm suggested. "Make sure all's good before Friday."

Finn nodded.

They swam down to Coded Archway. A coded door had been manufactured and constructed into the archway on the outside wall of the Creepy Cave. On it was a number touch panel for a code. It consisted of twenty-six numbers that insinuated that the code was a word, as there are twenty-six letters in the alphabet. The word then had been encrypted back to numbers. Storm punched in 1-25-12-8-26-2-25-12 the encrypted code for

TREASURE. The code had been discovered initially in an old copy of the novel 'Treasure Island' that belonged to Storm's father. The door clunked open, and Finn and Storm swam into the small space between the two doors they had named: Dome of Breath 2. Closing the door Finn punched in 16-26-19-8-21-11 the code for ISLAND on the panel of the second door. Another clunk sounded and the heavy door opened, leading to an outside sea well. Storm and Finn breathed air bubbles of relief. There was always a chance that whoever had installed the coded doors may at some point change the code!

Closing the grey aluminium door, they swam up the sea well, arriving in the bottomless rock pool. Emerging from the depth, cold fresh air and sea spray saturated them. The shrill chatter of gulls and the strong scent of seaweed filled the atmosphere. The sea well and entrance to the Creepy Cave, was situated at the west side of Puffin Island. A bottle green ocean, looked up at dark clouds with smatterings of blue that stared down at the island.

"Want to check the Key?" Finn asked.

Storm nodded and they swam back down to the bottom of the well. The temperature plummeting as they reached the bottom. Finn punched in the code for ISLAND and the door opened. They closed the door, hovering in the confined space. Pulling at the right side of the coded panel attached to the first door, it swung open on hinges to reveal a flat panel with four small key holes. Taking the ring of keys from her belt, Storm clicked the locks open revealing a large brass key. The Key to the Locked Room. Nodding at Finn who was frantically tapping his watch, she relocked and secured the key, replacing the panel. Punching in the code to TREASURE, the inner door opened, and they swam through to the Creepy Cave, pushing it shut behind them.

Storm's air gauge was flashing red. Panic and confusion shot through her. Why was her air supply so low? They had filled the cylinder the same way, numerous times before, and there should be five minutes of air left in her compact tank. Turning to warn Finn, she saw him swimming ahead at speed. Mere seconds of air were left. Breathing in the last of her air she swam past the blocking boulder, and along the short tunnel that seemed to have magically extended.

Panic filled her, as the last remanents of breath left her body. Why hadn't she swum upwards and broken surface in the Creepy Cave? Instead, she had taken what could prove to be a fatal risk. Black dots floated before her eyes. A vice like grip clutched her arm and she felt her mouthpiece ripped out and then oxygen, heady and delicious. The relief was incredible, likened only to dehydration and the first sips of fresh cold-water. The grip pulled her to the Dome of Breath 1 and then out into the Emerald Pool Chamber.

Finn helped her to the side of the pool. Clambering out he lifted her out like a child, plonking her on the blanket and wrapping her in a towel.

"What the bloody hell Storm!" he looked angry. "I had five minutes left. Did you even check your cylinder gauge before and whilst swimming?"

Storm nodded.

"I thought I had." Storm protested.

"Did you or not?" He demanded.

"I don't know Finn. I thought I had. Maybe I checked yours twice by mistake before we headed out. But no, not while we were swimming. I usually do. "

"And you think you're ok to stay down here alone! For a week!" Finn yelled. He was shaking with adrenaline and fear. "You usually do yes. But it only takes one mistake to die!"

"You're hardly one to have a go, Finn. You ran away from John the Psycho, and nearly drowned rowing to Puffin Island in the middle of a storm. How dumb was that! You're not my dad! Plus, you filled the cylinders, not me!"

"Yeah, I totally know that! And yeah, I'm an idiot I know that too." Finn poured them both out a drink. "I'm not trying to be like your dad, What the..."

"Well, I wouldn't bloody know what a dad is like, as he's never here!" Storm shouted back angrily.

"At least he's about sometimes! God knows where mine is!" Finn yelled back.

They glared at each other.

Finn's stomach growled loudly with hunger. The sound echoed through the chamber.

Finn and Storm burst out laughing. Tears streamed down Storm's cheeks.

"Messed up!" Storm said. Patting her aching sides. Their laughter bounced back, filling the cavern.

"Scared the shit out of me, Storm. Didn't mean to be a dick. Thought you'd drowned." He shook his head. "Turned around and you were like floating with vacant staring eyes." He shuddered. "Horror film material!"

"Totally. Carrie or worse!" Storm placed her hand on his shoulder. "I get it. Really. Was stupid and I should have double checked. Lesson learned. Sorry."

"I'm certain I filled the cylinders right." Finn said, his brow creasing with doubt. "It's possible the 'On' lever got caught and some of the air leaked out. Sorry I was stroppy. We both must be so careful. Double check everything from now on."

Storm nodded. The two of them were like cats with nine lives; but, at some point those lives would run out.

Mugs of tomato soup were poured and chicken and ham sandwiches, accompanied with grapes and crisps consumed. Finn took out the long-encrusted coral, he'd plucked from the Ghost Ship.

"Another one for the soapy bucket."

Storm nodded; her eyes gleaming with pleasure, she took his hand and squeezed it. Their treasure collection was growing. Another day of excitement on Puffin Island. However, the future was uncertain, and she wondered what the following week would bring.

CHAPTER 4
The Journey

The remainder of the days before adventure camp, were packed with English, Maths, Psychology, and Language lessons, coupled with chores, such as clearing tree mallow from the Puffins' nests on the south side of the island. Friday arrived in a flash! It was the day they were to leave Puffin Island and travel by train to Tyne Island in Dorset, on the south coast of England.

Storm and Finn sat eating breakfast in the dining room with Lily and Grandad Flint.

The smell of eggs, bacon and potato waffles filled the air. Finn tucked happily into his breakfast. Storm felt physically sick and only managed a mouthful of bacon and a sip of tea.

"You not eating that?" Finn eyed her discarded plate of food.

Storm shook her head.

"Can I have it?" Finn took her plate and ate the unwanted breakfast with enthusiasm. "Delicious Aunty Lily. You're the best."

"Thank you, Finn." Lily smiled with pleasure.

"Creep!" whispered Storm to Finn.

He grinned showing white even teeth.

"Looking forward to the trip?" asked Grandad Flint hopefully.

Dressed in jeans with a white shirt and tweed jacket he looked young and smart. He was physically fit and in good shape for fifty-three. His dark hair streaked with grey, was swept back. His musty aftershave mingled with the smell of cooked breakfast and Finn's deodorant.

"Sure Pops." said Finn, and Storm nodded.

He smiled with relief, but Finn could tell he was unconvinced. His dark blue eyes scrutinised Storm: but said nothing. He refilled the blue and white cups with steaming dark orange tea.

After breakfast they stood in the dining room with their rucksacks, ready to go.

"You can change your mind." Finn murmured. He looked tired, as he hadn't slept well the night before.

Storm nodded.

"I've thought about it a lot. Can't go Finn. Just can't."

"Can't" needs to become "can" Storm." Finn smiled weakly. He yawned loudly.

"Working on it. Can't - will be - can. Just not yet."

"Well, the email you sent to Tyne Adventures left it open…so if you get freaked out or decide to come, just jump on the train."

Storm nodded.

"Will you be, ok?" She rested her head on his arm for a moment.

"Yeah Storm. No need to worry about me. Journey's simple. Train Waverley to Kings Cross. Cab to Waterloo Station and train down to Poole which is …let me see." He checked the email on his phone. "It's in Dorset. Get a cab to Tyne quay and then over to Tyne Island on a boat. So nah, no big deal. I'll text you journey just in case. Fact I'll forward you this email too from them, about the week. Keep you in the loop."

"Cool." Storm tied her hair up into a messy bun on the top of her head with a black scrunchie.

Lily bustled into the room looking anxiously at Storm and Finn. Dressed in a black dress with tights and boots, her smoky eye makeup enhanced olive eyes that were so like her daughters. Her blonde hair hung down her back and expensive perfume clung to the air.

"All good?" she asked brightly.

"Ready to go." Finn said with equal enthusiasm. "You look stunning Aunty."

"Thanks Finn." She laughed. "Makes a change from scruffing around in painting clothes."

Storm glowered at her mother. Lily went to say something but changed her mind.

"Grandad Flint's taken our bags over to the mainland already. So, I'll lock up and meet you at the quay." She put a head scarf over her hair for the boat ride. "Wretched damp weather's making my hair kink."

Storm walked past her without a word. Reaching the door to the lighthouse tower she locked the door. She did not trust Hippy Clare not to go snooping.

Upon reaching the mainland, Grandad Flint hugged them goodbye.

"Have the best time. Love you both. Oh, to be young!" He said wistfully. "Wish I was going."

Walking to the row of garages painted black and white, situated behind the Boat House Cabin, he pressed a button on the remote control of his keyring. In response, the garage door hummed as it elevated. Disappearing inside, Grandad Flint, re-appeared moments later driving a gleaming silver Aston Martin. Tooting the horn, he waved exuberantly, roaring off into the distance, classical music blaring, leaving behind a trail of musical notes on the breeze. The garage door clicked shut.

"Boys and their toys!" Lily murmured shaking her head. "Thinks he's James Bond."

Finn shook with laughter.

"Pops is so totally cool."

They drove to Shelley station in Lily's old four-wheel drive. The train to Edinburgh pulled slowly into the station.

"It's just a week Storm." Lily said gently as the train inched slowly up the east coast.

"Hope you have a nice time with Dad and your painting thing goes well." Storm said quietly. "Say hi to him from me."

Lily looked relieved.

"Bit nervous about the exhibition but there's been a good response so far with ticket sales, so fingers crossed."

Arriving at Edinburgh Waverley, they checked the main screen for details of their journey. The Edinburgh to Kings Cross train was on time and leaving at 10.30 from Platform 2.

Lily hugged Storm tightly.

"Love you so much." she said.

"Love you too Mum and I'm sorry."

"Don't be daft Storm. Just want you to be happy."

Finn hugged his aunt.

"Good luck with the exhibition and say hi to Uncle Flint."

Storm and Flint boarded the London train and waved to a tearful Lily standing on the platform with her suitcase. Whistles blew, and the train moved off.

"First stop Berwick upon Tweed." said Finn. "Why don't you just come. They've got sea kayaking, sailing, army assault courses, camping out, bush craft. Everything you love."

Storm's olive eyes were huge and watery. Pulling the scrunchy from her bun. Her dark emerald hair hung around her face hiding the torrent of emotions surging within her. Tears threatened. A battle was literally raging inside. Half of her was desperate to go and do normal fun things and to be with Finn but her anxiety screamed at her. It was like a wall of paralysis.

"Next time I promise." She hated feeling selfish and worrying her mother and Finn; but anxiety was consuming her daily life. All the time no demands were made upon her she was ok. But the slightest change, especially being away from home, filled her with panic and horror. She simply wasn't ready for it.

"I hope so Storm." Finn ran his fingers through his thick dark hair. "The old saying: 'The definition of insanity, is doing the same thing over and over and expecting a different result'."

"Truth. That's cool. Did you make that up?"

"Nah, I wish. One of my old man's fav sayings. Albert Einstein said it. The German physicist. Did you know Einstein means one stone in English? Learnt that in German class."

"Wow well done Finn! You paid attention."

They both laughed.

"Seriously I'm impressed!" Storm smiled at him.

"Not the dumb ass people think." He grinned. "Just have zero attention span."

His long legs stretched out. Searching for leg room he kept nudging Storm's feet.

"Like ow. Finn long legs!" Storm's feet were pressed to the side of the carriage wall. "Have you grown again? I'm still five foot five."

"Six three now! Taller than my old man."

"No way!"

"Seriously. He won't know me."

"Wonder where he is."

Finn shrugged.

"Who knows. They have eyes everywhere, Special Forces, so you may get busted before you even get back to Puffin Island. Be careful!"

"Dad's always complaining about lack of resources, so sure they've got better things to do. We'll text all the time yeah."

"Defo. If we can't text for any reason, we let each other know. Like, I'll say: 'I've got an overnight campout' type thing, so you know. If we have radio silence more than three hours and no one's said anything then we know somethings up, yeah?"

"Totally."

The train slowed, and the conductor announced over the speaker system that they were shortly arriving at Berwick upon Tweed. Storm sat there. What if she just went to the camp with Finn? Did things differently. She wouldn't die. Her anxiety couldn't kill her. Maybe it was time, she faced it head on. The train pulled up at the station.

Storm kissed Finn on the cheek.

"Love you, Finn. You're like my brother."

"Same, but like sister. Love you, Storm." He hugged her.

Storm's mind had decided to go to Tyne Adventures, but her body had other ideas and she collected her bag and stepped off the train. Dark blue eyes connected to olive green, as the train departed from Berwick upon Tweed Station, London bound, moving slowly along the track. Storm stood watching until she lost sight of Finn.

Storm stood there in the grey drizzle of the early October morning. She knew Finn was disappointed. He'd clearly hoped that she would rise above her fear and go to camp with him; but it wasn't that simple. He understood why though, and that was some comfort to her.

"Weird." She murmured, referring to her own actions.

Taking a woolly hat out of the pocket of her thick wool-lined black hoody, she tucked her hair away, pulling the hood up. Dressed in black yoga pants and tanned army boots she looked slight and inconspicuous.

Storm had researched anxiety disorder extensively. Apparently, the mind in a fearful state creates the idea of dread and dangers that are unlikely to happen, causing a fight or flight response. Anxiety in this context, is 'made up fear' and the body responds by deciding whether to run or fight the proposed danger and sends out bursts of adrenaline, pure energy, to help deal with the situation. This energy if not used can cause feelings of sickness, aching limbs, dizziness, and stress.

However, in this instance, her mind had decided to go to camp but her body seemed to have said no!

It was as if her conscious mind that she used for thinking and making decisions in her daily life, had been taken over by her subconscious mind that carried all her emotions, past experiences, and dreams. Her sub-conscious mind seemed to be making the decisions. Interesting. Jenny her best friend would love to hear of Storm's self discovery as she was obsessed with becoming a counsellor when she left school.

Storm was now convinced that her mind was indeed broken. It had split. Now she needed to work out how to fix it. Glue it back together.

Her mind would have to wait however, as she was standing aimlessly on the platform at Berwick upon Tweed station at

11.30am in the rain, getting soaked. There was a bus that ran directly to Shelley. Her phone told her that the return journey would take two hours thirty-seven minutes.

Storm's stomach growled with hunger. Crossing the road to McDonalds, she ordered a big mac, fries, and a strawberry milkshake as a take-out to eat on the bus. The 253 bus, arrived on time, and Storm boarded, sitting purposely, on the right-hand side of the back seat where she had the best sea view. Taking a deep breath, she tried to ignore the mixed emotions that churned inside her. She felt scared, and guilty for leaving Finn.

"On bus to Shelley. Ok. Having a Big Mac." Storm texted Finn.

"Be careful cuz!" Finn text straight back. "And yum! I could so eat four of them right now!"

Storm grinned. His appetite was phenomenal.

The ice-cold strawberry milkshake gave her brain freeze. But the salty fries were comforting, and Storm enjoyed the meal. The bus hurtled along the A1 at top speed and the charcoal grey of the vast ocean stretched out for miles, broken only by the odd volcanic island and fishing trawler.

Day one of seven. If she managed to hide away for a week without her parents knowing, it would be a near miracle! One thing was certain, things seldom went according to plan.

CHAPTER 5
An Unwelcomed Guest

Storm was aware that leaving the bus at Shelley, was fraught with risk. Shelley was a small town, and everyone knew each other. However, there was a bus stop five miles outside the town, with a track opposite that led to a coastal route that would take her back to the Boat House Cabin.

The sky was a gloomy dark grey and rain lashed in pale dashes across the windowpane. Storm watched a lone rain drop separate from a pool of water that formed a line, slowly weaving its way down the glass, destination unknown. She could identify with the solitary raindrop.

'It's your own doing.' A nasty voice chattered in her brain and yes, the mean voice had a point. She could be laughing with Finn on the train right now. He would be nearing Leeds. Anxiety was the curse of her life.

The bus screeched to a halt at Cockburnspath. A lady, with a purple knitted hat and beige raincoat, head bowed against the vicious elements, boarded the bus grumbling. It was Mrs Mackay. Storm's Mother knew her! She worked at the biscuit factory in Cockburnspath and was an active member of Shelley bowling club. Her daughter was in the year below Storm at Shelley High School. Mrs Mackay parked her dripping trolley in the disabled and family space and plonked down on one of the blue and black lower seats. Fortunately, she didn't notice the dark figure lurking on the back seat. Already the journey was becoming tense and dangerous. Storm felt twitchy. How was she going to get past Mrs Mackay and leave the bus without being seen?

Anxiety pulsed in her stomach as they reached Dunbar. A large group of bedraggled people were waiting at the bus stop soaked by a torrential downpour. The smell of musty dampness entered the bus with them. Storm felt sick with nerves and wished she'd taken the train after all. This was far too stressful. Fortunately, Mrs Mackay got off the bus, making her way over to the supermarket situated across the road. A reprieve! The bus moved off. Storm decided to get off at the next bus stop. Her nerves were shredded to screaming point.

The bell pinged and Storm shot off the bus. Standing in a quiet residential street she crossed the road to the wooded area opposite. A brown sign pointed to the John Muir Way, a nature pathway that wound around the coastline, providing detours through fields and forests. Storm knew it well. There was also a bicycle trail, she and Finn had loved as children.

It occurred to her that the stress of avoiding attending Tyne Adventure camp was possibly worse than the trauma she would have experienced if she'd just faced her anxiety and gone to camp! She hadn't even reached Shelley yet and was already exhausted. The fact that she was even thinking this, could mean that she was making some progress to overcoming her anxiety. It was definitely, a positive. Maybe next year she would make it to camp. Lots of maybes. She thought, reflecting on Finn's words regarding changing: 'can't to can'. He was right and becoming wise in his old age.

Her phone pinged. It was a text from Finn.

"Bored. At Leeds. Had two bacon lettuce and tomato sandwiches, two steak slices, three packets of cheese and onion crisps, packet of bourbons and flask of hot chocolate. Where you at?"

"John Muir, Dunbar. Too many people on the bus. Weather's shit.

On way back to the cabin."

"Don't forget to check in Storm. Miss you cuz."

"Miss you too."

Storm sighed. Misery rained down on her as she walked towards the woods. Delving in her rucksack she pulled out a waterproof jacket.

"Come on." She muttered to herself. "Nearly there." She was determined to stay in a positive mind set.

The fast food consumed earlier, was making her feel sluggish and depressed. Gulping down water, she prepared for the trek, pulling the heavy rucksack onto her back. The twelve-mile dirt pathway wove through hundreds of wide mossy trees, their brown trunks sprouting vast branches that reached to the heavens. Millions of rustic leaves of orange, burgundy, green, yellow and reds wove into a tunnel like a vast colourful awning, sheltering her from relentless water cascading from the dark angry sky. Storm could smell salt on the breeze. The sea was near, and every step took her closer to home.

Walking in nature lifted her mood and Storm began to enjoy herself.

Her phone pinged. It was Finn.

"Dude got on at Peterborough. Says he's going to the adventure camp. Nooooo! He looks like thirty! Need to ditch! There's like no way, he's still at school!"

Storm laughed, she could just picture Finn's horror at being lumbered with a stranger.

"New pal." She typed.

"Oh helpful! He's like weird as. Trying to be all cool like."

"Just plug in and pretend to sleep."

"Yeah, said I'm stopping off in London before heading out to Dorset, will try and lose him."

The path was windy and long. Storm checked on the maps app, to make sure that she was going the right way. The track seemed to go on for ever.

Finn text:

"Kings X. Ditched the creepy dude."

His journey seemed to be going quicker than hers. Finally reaching the beach, the path thinned, and Storm squeezed through a mass of overgrown prickly orange bushes.

"Ouch! Ouch!" She detangled ginger gorse from her hair, before being greeted by a deserted rain drenched beach. A thin swirling sea mist hovered above miles of flat yellow sand. The black, white tipped ocean heaved in the distance. The tide was out. Sighing with relief, Storm relaxed.

Storm text Finn:

"Beach finally! Taken three hundred years!"

Glancing at her phone she was surprised to see it was five pm.

Clambering over purple, slippery rocks carpeted with green slime and limpets, Storm rounded a bend and squealed with excitement. Puffin Island appeared in the distance. The lighthouse stood majestically on top of the volcanic hill. The lamp flashing every thirty seconds into the dense fog.

The Boathouse Cabin and quay, separated by a natural rocky wall on either side, boasted a private beach. Trudging at speed, Storm arrived on Shelley Beach. Her legs aching from exertion. Surveying the area, Storm wandered up the path, to the Swift family car park and garages, where they'd waved Grandad Flint off earlier that day. It felt like a week ago to Storm.

An old green battered car sat where Lily's four-wheel drive had been. It had pink and yellow flower stickers on the back window and daisies hanging from the rear-view mirror. The car must belong to Hippy Claire!

Storm snorted with irritation. There was something off about

Claire, and she didn't trust her. Storm was soaked, despite the waterproof jacket, for the rainwater had found its way inside the neckline, seeping downwards to her clothing. However, she had arrived at the Boathouse Cabin undetected, so the first part of her mission was a success, be it an exceptionally long winded one. Making her way to the doorway of the boat house attached to the cabin, she froze as a light flicked on inside the bedroom at the back of the cabin. Placing her rucksack by the door, she crept over to the bedroom window, crouching below the sill.

The curtains were open and visibility for Storm was clear. Taking out her phone Storm switched the camera setting onto video and raised the phone up to the windowpane. The small device had less chance of being detected, than her head. Holding for about thirty seconds, she viewed the content.

The video showed the bedroom staring back at her and the flickering of a television screen in the living room. Then the bathroom door opened, and an overweight man walked out rubbing his bald head with a towel. He had a ginger beard, big white belly, black hairy chest and was dressed only in orange floral boxer shorts.

"Ew gross!" Storm whispered to herself.

Storm wished with all her heart that Finn was here. He would have found it so funny.

Attaching the video to messenger, she sent it to him.

"At the cabin and ew!" she chuckled to herself.

However, ugly image aside, she had a major problem. It had never occurred to her that the cabin would be occupied and with no contingency plan, there was a major flaw in her planning. There must always be Plan A, B and C for everything! The entrance to the Puffin Island tunnel was in the Boat House Cabin and worse, it was in the living room! What if the bald man decided to stay up for hours or even fall asleep on the sofa. Maybe he was Hippy Claire's husband. Apparently, he worked offshore a lot, and Storm had never met him. But why was he not with Hippy Claire, house sitting on Puffin Island, if that was the case?

"What the actual..." Finn text back. "Who's the ugly dude? And major ew! My eyeballs are burning at the sight!"

"No clue. Hippy Claire's husband? And yeah really!"

"Nearly in Dorset. Major prob Storm! What to do?"

What was she going to do? Storm's brow creased. The first option was to take the small boat out to the island. The weather was wet and murky, but the sea was calm and so the risk rowing over to Puffin Island was minimal. The patchy mist would hide her, and she could land on the west beach near the Cave of Boulders. There was a small flat inlet, where the gang's boat had been smashed to pieces months before during a violent storm. Storm shuddered. The image of the splintered boat and mangled engine didn't inspire confidence. If she followed option one, she could stay the night in the Cave of Boulders and sneakily enter the Light House the next day. The small boat would be discovered missing but what choice did she have.

Option two, she could wait in the Boat House until the man went to sleep and slink into the cabin. But what if he caught her in the act of lifting the old creaky trapdoor and Storm gave away the family secret! That was unthinkable! Knowledge of the underground tunnel that went from the Boathouse Cabin to Puffin Island was for family members only!

Even less attractive was the third option of spending the night in the boat house, as it was freezing outside, and even if she changed into dry clothes she would probably die of hyperthermia in the night. Plus, there was no guarantee that the man would venture out and leave the cabin the next day.

Pondering a solution, she considered that, if she set the boat adrift upon arrival on Puffin Island, the Coastguard would pick it up and return it thinking it hadn't been secured properly and had drifted. It wouldn't be the first time. Grandad Flint had lost the boat a few times in the past. The decision was made. She would wait until dusk then row over to the island. She'd text Finn upon her safe arrival.

CHAPTER 6
Finn the Hero

In stealth mode Storm crept back to the window of the boathouse cabin. Spying further on the bald man, Storm saw with relief that he was no longer in his boxer shorts, but instead, wearing a brown and white striped dressing gown. Opening a can of beer with a crack and a hiss, he settled himself on the sofa in front of the television. A quiz show flashed from the screen and the sound of canned laughter echoed throughout the boathouse cabin. Perhaps he was a security guard, hired by Grandad Flint to keep an eye on Puffin Island. Storm smiled. He didn't look capable of running too far or fast. In the worst case scenario, that she was discovered by him, she could easily outrun him.

Earlier that morning, Storm had sneaked to the lower cellar, removing the bunch of keys from behind the Keeper of Keys. They now sat securely in the zipped up inside pocket of her hoody. Storm inserted a silver key into the boathouse lock and turned it as quietly as possible. A click resonated and the grey wooden door opened. Water lapped quietly against the side of the quay. Locking the door behind her, Storm tiptoed gingerly across the timber planks, placing the heavy rucksack carefully into the small boat. Unclipping the swing doors, Puffin Island appeared through the dimness in the distance. Removing her waterproof jacket, she put on the orange life jacket before replacing the black coat over the top of it. Safety was paramount. Swapping the orange oars for black tipped spares, she stepped carefully into the boat, feeling it wiggle beneath her weight.

Untying the boat, she pushed off. Rowing carefully out of the boat house. The swing doors swung shut behind her. Her heart thudded inside her chest. It was a familiar journey to Puffin Island by sea, and one Storm had made hundreds of times before. Physically the journey was easy, but she was terrified of being caught in the act. Dipping the oars deeply into the sea for maximum propulsion she gently glided across the water with minimal sound. Soon the boathouse was a mere orange square of light. The air was chilly. Rain fell. White lines of froth cut through the inky blackness as the tide soared up the beach, now barely visible in the distance.

Upon her approach to Puffin Island, a glow illuminated from the living room window of the Light House, accompanied intermittently by a blast of brilliance, cast by the powerful lamp at the top of the lighthouse tower. How Storm longed for her cosy bedroom, situated just below. So cosy, snug and safe. Hopefully, Hippy Claire was stoned from the weed she smoked and was happily snoring her empty head off! Storm resented her being there. It was her home and yet she was the one sneaking around like a criminal, while Hippy Claire was warm and dry!

Heading to the west beach, Storm landed on the island on a small strip of flat sand hidden between jagged inky rocks. Placing the life jacket back into the locker of the small boat, she shoved the vessel back out to sea, watching it slowly bob away into the distance like a toy model boat on the tide. Dusk had transformed to darkness, and Storm decided to scout out the house. Climbing up the cliff, she ran crouched, to the living room. The French doors were open and the awning which resembled a makeshift conservatory that unfolded at the flick of a switch, had been activated. Storm thought it was ingenious the way the mechanism slid out from the building creating a metal frame and then the tarpaulin folded out over it. An orange flame flickered from the patio followed by a waft of majorana. Hippy Claire lounged in the shelter; smoking weed. Another flame flickered and the fire pit burst into life. Storm could make out her silhouette, laying on the lounger, chattering into her mobile phone, cackling with laughter.

It was the perfect opportunity to enter the Light House via the front door. Storm moved carefully backwards. A loud crack reverberated as her foot snapped a rotten arched stick. Hippy Claire visibly jumped. Storm froze for a second, then threw herself flat onto her belly. Swathed in black she hid her face into the earth.

"If there's someone there. I'm armed!" Hippy Claire shrieked hysterically into the blackness. A beam of frantic torchlight spun at random.

Startled, an owl flew from the treetop near Storm. Passing Hippy Claire, it screeched back at her. Screaming Hippy Claire fled back into the house. Satisfied that the owl was the intruder, she reappeared, moments later. Lighting a cigarette, she settled back down.

"Creepy weird place." Claire sobbed, blowing out clouds of putrid smoke like an old dragon. "I'm armed, I say. Armed!" She yelled into the night from the safety of her lounger.

Armed! What an idiot! Storm thought scornfully. Hippy Claire would probably shoot herself if given a weapon. She was pathetic! Storm lay cold and wet in the mud. The safest idea for now was to go back to the Cave of Boulders. She could light a fire. The night was misty and Hippy Claire was already burning a fire so any trace wouldn't be detected.

On her front Storm crawled: left arm left leg, then right arm right leg, low, back to the cliff edge and dropped down to the sand below. Using the torch from her phone to guide her way, she removed boulders and clambered into the familiar cave. Moving the chimney boulder to the side she created a gap for the smoke to trail out. Replacing the other stones at the entrance, Storm lit the lanterns, filling the cave with cheer. A big pile of kit sat at the back of the cave next to the kindling and Storm started in alarm. Gangsters had hidden a stash here once before, if they were using the island again then Storm's one haven was destroyed. Moving closer and shining the white beam on it, she laughed. Her tired mind was playing tricks on her.

Wonderful forward-thinking Finn had not only left supplies: 'just in case,' but also kit including a wet suit and air cylinder.

"Clever, clever Finn." Storm smiled, laughing with relief.

Checking her phone, she saw four messages from him.

"What you gonna do?" Text one.

"You, ok?" Text two.

"Arrived on Tyne Island. It's ok." Text three.

"Text me!" Text four.

"On PI and all good. In C o B and I have no words. Thanks Finn! Absolute life saver!" Storm replied.

Finn texted back immediately.

".... Sake! Sharing a room with the creepy dude! Noooooooooooo! Might join you! Seriously not happy!"

Storm sighed.

"Aw. Hugs." Storm texted back.

"No way he's like my age and all hairy. Totally is not. Text sooner Storm! Remember the comms plan. I was creeped out - hearing nothing."

"Will do. Same to you."

Lighting a fire in the rocky grate, Storm stripped off her cold wet clothes and changed into dry ones, laying the wet items over the black slate near the fire. The flames crackled merrily, hungrily devouring the diet of twigs and small logs. Snuggled into a thermal shirt, fleecy track trousers and hoody, Storm wore cosy socks. Warmth and light filled the small haven.

Included in the supplies was a small camp stove, pan, litres of water and flasks. The large plastic containers, previously used for drugs or counterfeit money by the gang, were now packed by Finn with tins of tomato soup, beans, bread, cheese spread, milk, and hot chocolate. There was also a ground sheet and military issue sleeping bag. Finn was leading by example. Storm should have thought ahead. Her plan for her secret week on Puffin Island was full of more holes that a pasta strainer!

Putting a milk pan onto the stove to boil, Storm added chocolate powder and made up a flask. Rinsing out the pan she added tomato soup and piled a thick layer of cheese spread onto the seeded bread. Dipping it into the steaming soup she wolfed down her meal. Storm was famished. If it hadn't been for Finn, she would be sitting in the Cave of Boulders, hungry and miserable with limited fuel for the fire. She hoped he was alright. He sounded fed up and cross.

The creepy dude sharing Finn's room, kept coming into her mind. Finn was a great judge of character. If he didn't like someone it was because they were toxic or fake. He did not suffer fools. However, he could look after himself. Storm wasn't doing such a great job. Sipping hot chocolate, her eyes felt tired, suddenly she felt overwhelmed with fatigue.

Tomorrow, if Hippy Claire showed no signs of movement, she would tidy the cave and then dive down to the bottom of the sea well, to the coded archways and enter the underground world that way. Adding fuel to the fire Storm climbed into the cosy sleeping bag. Warm contentment was her companion. She was safe at home on Puffin Island. Closing her eyes, she slept.

CHAPTER 7
Dark Clouds Gather

Awaking at six am, Storm stretched. Warm and cosy in her sleeping bag, only her face peeped out. The air was cold and crisp. The crash of the tide echoed and tinkled outside the wall of the cave, casting pebbles and seashells up the beach, before dragging them back into the froth. After a peaceful and deep night's sleep, Storm felt refreshed and optimistic. Grabbing her phone, the battery was on twenty five percent. There was a portable charger that ran from batteries, in the storage room that contained the military kit and diving equipment. However, was it still there? Finn or even her dad or Grandad Flint could have taken it to use. The best course of action was to leave her phone outside the back door of the kitchen, dive down to the well, enter through the coded archways, and creep up, through the cellar to collect it. She texted Finn. It was too risky to enter the house through the front door.

"You, ok?" she texted.

"About to be arrested for murder." He replied. "Dude snored like a pig. All night! And I mean ALL NIGHT!"

Storm smiled, climbing reluctantly out of her snug cocoon. Putting a pan of water on the stove for tea she bit into a chocolate and peanut protein breakfast bar. It was a bit chewy but tasty and Storm needed energy.

"WYD today?" she text Finn.

"Sea Kayaking. U?"

"Hippy Clare is everywhere here. Can't use front door like a normal person, going in through sea well! Low battery so need to charge it. What's camp like?"

"Room's nasty. Woke up and thought I was in jail. Old plastic mattress and prison bunk beds. Dodgy roommate."

"What room you in?"

"Blue 5, blue block. Names on door Locke and Dunn."

"That the dudes' name?"

"Yeah. Adrian Dunn. 'I prefer Aidie!' Idiot!"

Storm laughed.

"Text at lunch?"

"Roger that."

Quickly tidying the cave, Storm glanced at her phone. It was now six thirty. It would have been wise to set her alarm earlier for it was likely that Hippy Clare would be awake. Storm sighed. Sneaking about undetected, was proving to be hard work. If she'd awoken at four am, she could have moved about Puffin Island freely. Forward thinking was a skill learnt through making mistakes. It didn't come naturally to Storm, at fourteen.

Moving the boulders from the entrance, she poked her head out of the cave. Greyness enveloped her. Clouds of vapour swirled around Puffin Island. The haar, or sea mist common to Shelley, descended. Rain pelted down in a steady flow. Her clothes from the day before were dry. Shaking them free from sand, Storm dressed in a thermal vest, thick hoody, and yoga pants, adding trainers. Quickly setting the fire for her return, she glanced around her, trying to think clearly.

The bald man had really mucked up her plans. Clothing was becoming an issue. It had been her intention to leave some in the Locked Room where she'd planned to sleep, but she had been so stressed about the adventure camp, the thought had disappeared out of her mind. There were two sets in the cave of boulders and the rest were in her bedroom in the lighthouse tower. The temperature was cold for October, especially underground, and she couldn't stay in a wetsuit or take her existing clothing via the sea entrance. Stuffing her army boots, change of clothes and phone into a thick plastic bag she found in a crate, she left her sanctuary. It was now six forty-five.

Cursing the pitter-patter of the rain on the plastic, Storm sealed the entrance to the Cave of Boulders, and crept along the beach, up to the clifftop, and along the strip of grass to the mini forest. Hiding behind a tree, she viewed the Light House. A glow shone from the guest bedroom. Hippy Clare was awake! Storm sighed with frustration. Bending low she ran at speed from the woods to the back of the house. Apart from the light there was no sign of life. Bag in one hand, her hand shook as she fished out the bunch of keys from her hoody pocket. She inserted the key into the kitchen door lock. It failed to turn. Storm would have been surprised if it had. There was another key in the inside door lock, and so hers was ineffective! Turning the door handle she pushed. The door was locked! It had been worth a try.

Soaking wet and freezing cold, Storm's teeth chattered. Leaving the bag by the door she turned and ran back to the Cave of Boulders. Changing into the wet suit, she laid her sodden clothes out to dry on the rocks in the cave.

Once again, she left the cave, this time sprinting to the rockpool at the end of the strip of beach. The sand felt cold and sharp on her bare feet as the beach was full of tiny broken shells and random strips of thick dark brown seaweed. Carefully making her way over a row of slippery grey and yellow speckled rocks, she inserted the mouthpiece, checked the air gauge, turned on the air and dived down the sea well to the coded door below. The water was bitterly cold, but the wetsuit insulated her. Punching in the ISLAND code. She entered Dome of Breath 2. Entering the code for TREASURE she entered the Creepy Cave. Breaking the surface she shone her torch around, gleaning comfort from the now familiar sight of the Ghost Ship that had once frightened her.

Swimming past the fallen boulder she passed through the archway and Dome of Breath 1 into the Emerald Pool Chamber. It was pitch black. Storm usually lit lanterns and candles upon entry from the tunnel entrance. Clambering out of the pool she lit the candles with the matches she'd left in the chamber, congratulating herself on her foresight in that area at least. The illumination was welcome. Storm needed to move quickly. Once she knew Hippy Claire's routine and movements, she would be ok. At present, Storm was stressed about the bag she'd left outside the backdoor, terrified that it would be discovered!

Unlocking the sealed door, she made her way down the short passage, up the slate steps and with exertion moved the slab upwards. Storm was now in the tunnel, taking care to close all doors behind her just in case Hippy Claire caught her. Flashing the torch around her, she noticed drips of water leaving a trail. Diverting to the storage room containing the linen, she dried herself with one of the rough towels on the rack. Perhaps Finn had left supplies in the Locked Room? She would check after retrieving her phone. Fear at being caught prevented her collecting the key to the Locked Room until she had safely retrieved the bag.

Paranoia was building by the second. Sprinting back along the zig-zagging tunnel she came to the end, directly beneath the Light House. Climbing the icy metal rungs, she took the keys unlocking the thick stone slab. This set off the mechanism. It slid down and back. Storm removed the thin wooden plywood covering. Now for the trapdoor that led to the lower cellar. Clicking open the locks she pushed the door open a crack. It felt heavier than usual. Potato sacks must have been placed on it. A shape appeared meowing loudly. It was Marmalade her ginger cat. Could the day get any worse! Picking up her scent he mewed near the trap door.

Claire's shrill voice sounded from the kitchen.

"Yuck this stuff stinks! Marmalade! Breakfast!" A clattering of plates and the distant meowing of Marmite her black cat. Marmalade torn between Storm and food sniffed around the gap where Storm had lifted the trapdoor a fraction. Hippy Claire flicked on the light of the first cellar.

"Come on wretched cat." Hippy Claire yelled sounding irritable. "Creepy down here!"

Her phone rang and Marmalade zoomed off to eat his breakfast.

"Yeah, slept ok. You?" A pause. "All quiet. Yeah, will go stir crazy. Pub sounds great Aren't you s'posed to be working?" Another pause, then Hippy Claire's cackle. "Nah no one will know. Easy money! Bath, then be over bout twelve…ok make it eleven. Love ya!" Claire spoke loudly into the phone.

Footsteps. Then silence.

Storm raised the trapdoor tentatively and the potato sacks slid off. Squeezing through the space between the door and the floor, the solid wood lent on her leg and turning Storm lifted it, closing it quietly. Creeping slowly through the dimness, she ventured up the steps to the next cellar. Hippy Claire had left the light on in the first cellar. So much for caring for the environment, Storm thought scornfully. It was a great help to Storm, however. She'd also left the kitchen door open that led to the cellars and Storm could feel the heat from the house flowing down.

Storm could have waited until Hippy Claire went over to the mainland, but she was too anxious. Inching her way to the back door she turned the key in the inside lock and opened the door. Marmalade appeared from nowhere and rushed out!

"Damn it!" Storm cursed quietly.

Grabbing the drenched plastic bag, Storm closed the door and re locked it. Water dripped all over the floor. So now there was a cat that could open doors on its own, and a trail of water! Well maybe it was Hippy Claire's turn to be freaked out. Hopefully then she might leave. Taking a tea towel, she wiped the bag and the floor before putting it back on the radiator. Eyeing the key in the back door Storm pocketed it. She now had access via the kitchen. Let Claire wonder about that too!

Marmalade sat meowing pitifully outside the French doors leading to the living room. He was disgusted by the water that fell from the sky, soaking his orange coat so it formed spikes like a punk rocker. The door opened and Claire appeared in her dressing gown. Lighting a cigarette, she shook her head with confusion.

"How the hell did you get out?"

Storm grinned. Glancing around the kitchen she checked she'd left no trace and disappeared back into the cellar. Opening the freezer, on the way, she grabbed a homemade quiche and bag of cheese and onion pasties. They would be thawed by lunchtime.

Down in the tunnel once more she fished out her phone. There was a message from her mother hoping that Storm was enjoying camp and saying how proud she was that she'd gone, adding that she'd sold five paintings already! Lily had obviously forgotten about radio silence! Guilt and treachery drummed her belly. Nothing from Finn yet. Hunger rumbled through her. Storm decided to put her phone on charge. Plugging it into the battery pack charger, she left it under the trap door to collect later and ventured back up the tunnel to the Emerald Pool Chamber.

Finn was right, they really did need to install heating underground. Next task was to check out the Locked Door. Shivering she inserted the mouthpiece and plunged back into the water. Punching codes into the Coded Door she retrieved the Key from behind the panel. Storm had become so accustomed to Finn being by her side, she felt quite lonely. Swimming back through the Emerald Pool Chamber she opened the Locked Door entering the room beyond. It was sparse with just the camp bed and a sleeping bag and wardrobe within. Finn had left an envelope with a wad of fifty-pound notes and a pair of cosy socks. The socks were a joke because when he'd first arrived on

Puffin Island, he'd complained that his feet were permanently freezing. Storm looked around happily. It was a safe and secure place to spend the night. She placed her change of clothes in there and relocked the door.

Her stomach demanded hot food! Returning the key to the secret panel in the coded door, Storm made her way back to the Cave of Boulders, emerging in the rock pool. The weather was dull, but the rain had ceased and the haar lifted. Speeding back to the cave, Storm was thankful she'd set the fire and stood in front of the dancing flames enjoying the heat. Peeling off the wet suit, she dressed in her final set of dry clothes. Heating mushroom soup she made a cheese spread and crisp sandwich and a flask of hot chocolate. Her stomach growled with appreciation, and she ate with relish. The hot chocolate was like heaven in a mug as the heat spread through her. Hot, sweet, and rich.

Next on the agenda was to spy on Hippy Claire to make sure she left the island. Storm could enter the house now via the back door to the kitchen which was a massive relief. The house would be her own, for at least a couple of hours. She was desperate for a steaming shower. It felt like years since Finn had gone to camp but it was only a day. Saturday seemed endless. Maybe she'd call him later.

CHAPTER 8
Radio Silence

Storm lay flat on her stomach high up on the south-west point of the cliff top, watching Hippy Claire sauntering down the quay chattering into her phone. She wore a long-flared patchwork skirt of green and purple with a paisley pattern, a white top and a tan leather waistcoat. Her skirt blew up in the wind showing off purple tights with daisies tucked into brown ankle boots. Her frizzy mousey brown hair flew around her face in wild abandonment, mingling with the beige glitter scarf tangled around her scrawny neck.

Climbing into the motorboat she headed off towards the mainland. Storm sighed with relief, as Hippy Claire became a spec in the distance. Standing up she walked around to the kitchen door and let herself in. Marmite and Marmalade meowed in greeting. Storm fed them some biscuits and filled up their water bowl as it was dry. Hippy Claire really was useless. Collecting her phone and charger from beneath the trapdoor in the cellar, she went to the Lighthouse Tower, shutting and locking the door behind her. It was so good to be home. It felt like such a long time since she'd last stood in her bathroom. A text pinged from Finn.

"Bored! Lesson on how to Kayak sensibly, how not to capsize plus the dangers of sea kayaking. Yawn! Creepy dude keeps staring. Something off about him. Practical this afternoon. Call you at 5. Ya good?"

"Yeah good. Have fun." Storm text back. Taking a plug, she charged both her phone and the battery pack.

Chilled to the bone Storm ran a bath. Luxuriating in hot steaming water her body began to thaw out. Washing her hair, she pondered Finn's comments. The 'creepy dude' was probably just being friendly, or he might even have a crush. After John the Psycho, his Mum's ex -boyfriend, Finn had become guarded, to whom he let into his life.

Storm dressed in clean dry clothes and wound her hair up into a bun. Checking through her social media she nearly made the mistake of commenting on her friends' feed! Holly had won yet another gymnastic competition. She was so focused, and it was a massive achievement. Silly mistakes like that would blow Storm's cover.

A cheerful baby blue sky gleamed through her round bedroom windows. Storm had no idea how long Hippy Claire would be absent. At two thirty there was still no sign of her. Storm packed a bag containing the battery pack plus warm blankets, towels and food and dropped it down into the tunnel.

Wandering around the island, she planned her week, deciding that it would be fun to explore the Ghost Ship further. It was nice to finally relax and get organised. Sitting on a flat rock, she gazed out to sea. Dark clouds were forming, spreading fast like spilt paint, wiping out the powder blue. The sea began to writhe, becoming wilder with each breaker that rolled inland, crashing onto the black crag and casting white spray high up into the air.

The sky blackened. The sea turned iron grey. Rain fell. Storm checked her weather app. Rain one hundred percent for the rest of the day and all week. The wind not to be outdone howled a ghostly tune, tugging at her hood. Storm looked out towards the mainland. There was no way Hippy Claire would be able to travel back to the island in this weather. A major storm was on its way.

Running over to the west of the island, she made sure the boulders were all in place, sealing the Cave of Boulders from the elements. The waves were enormous, zooming up the beach but just falling short of the cave. Even Storm who was proficient with boats, would never attempt a journey in this wild sea. Letting herself in the back door she checked she had left no trail and returned to her bedroom in the lighthouse tower. Lying on her bed she decided to rest and enjoy the warmth while she could. She loved her round bedroom. Her bed sat in the middle of the floor. There were posters of rock bands on the walls and her duvet and pillowcase set were skull and cross bones. She'd painted the doors of the built-in wardrobe black, and a fluffy white rug sat on the gleaming oak floorboards. It was perfect.

Her eyes closed, and Storm slept.

BANG! CRACK! RUMBLE! Awaking with a start, thunder echoed loudly above. The house was in darkness illuminated intermittently by the lighthouse lamp. The storm raged noisily outside. Whining, whistling wind, growling menacingly. In panic Storm sat up, she couldn't believe she'd fallen asleep. Looking out of her bedroom window, she saw that the quay was empty, just white froth shooting up into the air. Hippy Claire had not returned. A light shone in the distance in the direction of the Boat House Cabin. Storm's fuddled brain was trying to make sense of the situation. She was disorientated. What on earth was the time?. Her phone said eight pm. She had literally slept for hours. There were no messages on her phone. She checked Finn's last message. He'd said he would call at five pm. Storm frowned. Three hours late. Unease sat happily in her belly nudging anxiety to wake up.

She texted Finn.

"Fell asleep. Are you ok?"

It was supposed to be radio silence at the camp. If he had been caught using his phone it may have been confiscated. Finn mentioned that he thought they weren't that strict and that the rule was a guide, for the purpose of giving young people a chance to grow, without parental involvement. Checking his location, he still appeared to be at Tyne Adventure Camp. It was too soon to worry. He may simply be busier than he thought.

Storm slipped on her trainers and went to the bathroom, dousing her face with freezing water. Heading to the kitchen she rolled down the blackout blinds and switched on the under-cabinet lights. In the fridge Storm discovered a plate of cooked chunky chicken and salad covered in clingfilm. It must be Hippy Claire's dinner. Storm frowned. Her mum mentioned that Hippy Claire was a vegetarian. Apparently not! What an actual fake! Placing a chicken and ham pie in the oven, with chips, she made some hot chocolate.

The cats, awoken by the smell of cooking, arrived in the kitchen meowing, and butting her legs. Storm took the chicken from Hippy Claire's dinner plate and gave it to Marmite and Marmalade who were delighted. She replaced the stolen meat with strips of cheese.

"The weed ain't the only thing messing with your brain girl!" she said out loud laughing to herself at the mind games created for Hippy Claire's benefit. Finn was right though. A week was a long time to spend alone!

The hot meal and empty house were a bonus. The pie tasted divine. If the house smelt of cooked food the next day when Hippy Claire returned, Storm really didn't care. The poor cats would have starved left in her care.

Checking her phone there were still no messages.

Storm decided to head to the tunnel and venture along to the Boathouse Cabin. If she removed the slab near the entrance, beneath the trapdoor hidden by a rug, she may well be able to hear what was going on.

Pulling on an extra jumper, Storm headed down the tunnel shining the powerful beam around her. The yellow circular light bobbed in the blackness. A feeling of impending doom nagged at her. Finn had been so adamant that if they couldn't contact each other, they must say. Yet he was the one who had failed to do so.

At the tunnels end, Storm carefully unlocked the slab. It too, was set in a metal frame and dropped down and slid back. Stepping up onto an iron rung, Storm's head was just below the trap door. She could hear voices belonging to Hippy Claire and a male voice that must be the bald man.

"Good so far." Hippy Claire slurred. The sound of glasses clinking and liquid pouring. "Home and dry! In the clear I reckon!"

"Yeah. I'm the security here. You're house-sitting! We're the trusted pals of the Swifts." He laughed loudly.

"My sister wants to buy a wee cottage in Wales. Sound like a plan?"

"Nah, too cold. Somewhere warm. Spain. Costa del Sol. Sun, sea and still get a fish supper."

Hippy Claire cackled with laugher.

"Shhh walls 'ave ears and all that. Creepy bloomin place that island. Dunno why anyone would want to live there. An' that spoiled brat. Give me strength! Was worried I would get lumbered with her!"

"Aye as you say. Walls 'ave ears. And yeah would have been a pain but could 'ave made life easier..."

"Got five Corries on catch up." The familiar whine of the start of the soap opera blasted. Hippy Claire and the bald man fell silent.

Storm's legs began to shake. The spoilt brat reference was obviously aimed at her, and the creepy place was Puffin Island. But what did Hippy Claire mean when she said they were in the clear? Was she refering to the house sitting and security jobs and the fact that they were not actually doing the jobs they were paid to do, or was she refering to something more sinister? Unanswered questions bounced around her brain. The talk of houses in Wales and Spain and their relocation seemed out of context in the conversation. It sounded as if they were receiving money and a lot of it. Whatever it was, Hippy Claire's sister was involved. Storm carefully replaced the slab. Crouching at the bottom of the tunnel, fear flooded through her. Desperate to talk to Finn, she went back along the tunnel towards the kitchen. Reaching the Emerald Pool Chamber, her phone pinged. There was a phone signal in that area for some bizarre reason.

It was not Finn! It was a missed call from her friend Jenny and a text asking if she fancied meeting up when she got back from camp. Storm called Finn. No answer!

Worried Storm returned to the kitchen and made herself a hot chocolate. Sitting at the breakfast bar, she typed Tyne Adventures into the search engine. The range of activities were vast, and Finn was right, she would have enjoyed it. Clicking on the team that ran the adventure camp, she scrolled through them. The Director: A woman with sandy hair and glasses. Head of Activities: Tall, dark, and physically in good shape. Senior Administrator:

"Oh no!" Staring back at her was the spitting image of Hippy Claire. Jane Dunn, Senior Administrator. Mousy hair. Pale blue eyes. Job role: Welfare. Problem solving. Bookings and general admin!

What on earth was going on? Storm wondered. In a way it made sense. Hippy Claire may have recommended Tyne Adventures to Lily, Storm's Mother, because her sister worked there. As her Mum's friend, it wasn't odd that Hippy Claire was house sitting and her bald husband was guarding Puffin Island. What was strange was that Finn hadn't responded to her text or calls, plus, the overheard conversation and the obvious hostility in their voices towards her family and the Puffin Island!

Storm wondered whether to call her mum. But she would have hell rain down on her for not attending camp and for the fraudulent email! Plus, she didn't know why Finn was being quiet. Storm needed to think. She had no idea what to do! If she didn't hear from him by morning, there was a good chance that he was in trouble. She needed to come up with a plan and fast!

CHAPTER 9
A Phone Call and A Journey

Storm nervously chewed the side of her thumb. Punching in the telephone number for Tyne Adventures she heard it ringing, then a change of tone as the call was automatically diverted.

"Tyne Adventures out of hours emergency service. How may I help you?" The voice was female and lethargic.

In order to impersonate her Aunt Molly, Storm put on a deep well -spoken tone. Her own voice was softer with a mere hint of a Scottish accent.

"Good evening. I'm trying to get hold of my son Finn Locke. He's staying at the centre this week."

There was a pause.

"And you are?"

"Mrs Locke. Finn's Mother." Storm made a face, obviously she was his mother as she had referred to him as her son.

"Hold on one moment."

"Thank you." Storm waited. Distorted classical music droned. The woman returned.

"We don't allow phone calls from parents Mrs Locke. Did you not realise?" Her tone was whining and patronising.

"Yes, I know but this is important. Whom am I speaking to?"

Another pause.

"Ms Dunn. I'm the Senior Administrator." The voice divulged reluctantly. "Lights out, is at ten pm Mrs Locke. He'll be asleep. Can't it wait until tomorrow? Do I really have to go and wake him?" Stern disapproval rung in her ear.

"Yes. It's very important. It's an emergency!" Storm snapped snootily. The line went dead. What a cheek! Storm was furious. Redialling, it rang and rang. No answer.

Storm had purposely left the tunnel open for quick access, as she was in the house alone and protected from the outside world by stormy weather. Sprinting to the lower cellar, she scrambled down the rungs in haste, racing at top speed back down the zig-zagging tunnel. Up the slopes she panted and down again until she reached the cabin. Hastily sliding back, the slab once more, she listened beneath the trapdoor.

"No worries Jane. Molly's at some rehab...sure it was her?... it was...nah no bother, she's probably just having a funny turn an' got hold of a 'phone. Don't worry about it...." Hippy Claire cackled with laughter. "Cut her off...!" more laughter. "Nah sis Nah don't fuss. Call you in the morning...watching Corrie."

"What's all that 'bout?" The bald man's voice. He belched loudly.

"Jane said Molly called for Finn Locke. She's neurotic so probably just had a weird turn as I said. She's at some rehab place, at the moment, on Mull."

"Nothing to bother 'bout. You sure?!

"Yeah." Hippy Claire said confidently.

A series of loud farts echoed.

"You dirty.... yuck that stinks!" Hippy Claire shrieked.

Cackles of laughter sounded as the TV sprang to life once more.

Storm replaced the slab and ran back down the tunnel. Sitting in the kitchen with her head in her hands her brain was whirling. Logically, broken down, everything could be deemed as normal. There was no actual evidence of foul play, but intuition told her otherwise. The phone call was suspicious. Why had Jane Dunn phoned her sister about 'Molly's' phone call, unless there was something odd going on. This coupled with the previous overheard conversation, was grim. Warning bells were chiming loudly in Storm's brain, like the bells of Notre Dame, alerting her to trust her instincts.

Tomorrow Hippy Claire would return to Puffin Island. Storm had to shelve her anxiety and find out what happened to Finn. It was nearly eleven pm and there were still no texts or calls from him! Tomorrow she would make the trip to Poole in Dorset and travel over to Tyne Island. Finn had given her emergency money, and this was apt in the circumstances. Her cousin may currently be fast asleep in Room Blue 5 oblivious to her anguish; but then again, he might be in mortal danger willing her to act. Her intuition screamed it was the latter.

Months before, Finn's dad: Captain Josh Locke, Special Forces, had been involved in a secret operation. Undercover. He'd infiltrated, and set up, a gang of dangerous organised criminals and taken a substantial amount of money from them. The gangsters were involved in counterfeit money and although some of them had been killed during the operation, it was likely fellow gang members were intent on revenge, desperate to recover their money. Storm had an uneasy feeling that Finn's silence had something to do with this. Finn was so aware of her anxiety issues, there was no way he would ever leave her to worry unnecessarily. Storm was convinced that Hippy Claire, the bald man, and Rude Jane were being paid by the gang and all working together.

Storm felt sick to her stomach, as she prepared for the trip. Taking inspiration from Finn's forward thinking, she decided to cover every eventuality, however extreme it appeared. Sitting on her bed in her cosy round bedroom, she checked off her list. This was serious, maybe a case of life or death and they could afford no mistakes. Wet suits and air cylinders were packed in the black rucksack retrieved from the Cave of Boulders. Storm had taken care to tape the 'off' button down to prevent air leakage. Containing just ninety minutes of air they were small and not too heavy. The thick large plastic bags from the crates in the cave were used to line the rucksack, to keep the contents dry should they, by some stroke of evil fate, end up in the sea.

She placed her and Finn's passports in a double freezer bag, adding a thousand pounds in fifty-pound notes from their emergency fund. Storm tucked their lifeline into the zipped inside pocket of her yoga pants. She was aware of how fortunate they were to have this money, given to Finn by his dad. Josh had left it for him in the Locked Room just before he vanished, for a second time. The Swift's had not always been wealthy. If they were still living in army accommodation with just her dad's military salary to support them, she'd be lucky to have ten pounds to her name.

Placing her purse into the inside pocket of her thick black wool lined hoody, Storm packed clothes and food. Cheese and onion pasties, protein bars, chicken mayonnaise sandwiches, sausage rolls, crisps and bottles of water were all carefully tucked in. The rucksack was heavy!

Venturing back down to the storage room, she sifted through the military kit taking spare batteries for the torch. Rummaging through her dad's old Bergen, she pulled out a tool belt. It contained wire cutters, a metal scoop that folded down resembling a small spade used for weeding the garden. A penknife hid in another pouch with all sorts of gadgets, including a bottle opener. A squashed tomato pasta ration pack and a bar of chocolate sat in another. Storm grinned. Cigarettes and matches, were in a smaller one. Storm frowned. In the final pouch she discovered wire, a small fold up saw and money. Two hundred pound in sterling and four hundred Euros. Storm took the belt. She adjusted it and wrapped it around her waist underneath her hoody.

Returning to the kitchen. It was now two am. Catching sight of her reflection in the ornate kitchen wall mirror Storm realised she had a problem. She looked fourteen and the last thing she wanted was to be picked up by the police.

Entering her mother's gleaming grey marble bathroom, she borrowed her makeup. Applying black eyeliner, a small amount of brown eyeshadow, mascara and eyebrow pencil, face powder and a mild red lipstick, she pouted! Storm the model. Wow! she did look good. Storm was surprised at the transformation. The lipstick was too much so she wiped it off and put on a lip salve with a faint shimmer instead. Weaving her hair into a thick dark green plait, she tidied away any evidence of her being there. She was prepared for battle.

Storm gasped and screamed in horror.

"No!" she yelled.

Her mind had finally registered that she had no boat!

The small boat she'd arrived in, Storm had cast out to sea. It had probably been returned to the Boathouse by the Coastguard, by now, but it wasn't on Puffin Island! Hippy Claire had taken the motorboat over to the mainland. Storm couldn't believe it!

"You total moron!" She screamed into the hallway. Marmalade who was sitting washing himself on the hall table gave her a startled look.

Now the only means she had to get to the boathouse was through the tunnel and Hippy Clare and her husband were both sleeping in the cabin! Storm would literally be walking straight into enemy camp! Plus, the rucksack was cumbersome and there was no way she'd get that through the trapdoor quietly. She could just imagine herself banging and crashing around the Boathouse Cabin waking them up and the hell that would follow!

Storm fed the cats, emptying a large pile of biscuits onto a plate. The revised plan was to sneak into the Boathouse Cabin, while the enemy was asleep, journey back to Puffin Island in the motorboat, collect her kit and head off down the coast to Dunbar. At the Harbour, she'd moor the boat and cross to the railway station where she'd board the train to London Euston. Storm sighed. The whole point of the last few days had been to avoid the stress and anxiety of traveling down to Tyne Adventure Camp, but ironically 'life' full of strange curves and bends had decided that it was her destiny to go to Dorset to Tyne Island, whether she liked it or not.

The storm had temporarily ceased, and sliver stars shone through the blackness. A million souls twinkled down, watching the strife that had become her life. Dumping the rucksack on the quay with her boots and socks, a gentle breeze tugged her plait. The rain stopped. Returning to the house, Storm locked the door to the lighthouse tower, kissed both cats and entered the tunnel once more. This time she closed the entrance in the cellar. On her feet she wore slippers as the intention was to enter through the trapdoor with bare feet as this was her best chance to move about quietly.

Leaving the slippers in the tunnel, she climbed the rungs. They felt ice cold and dug into her feet. Storm carefully opened the slab at the end of the passageway. The task ahead was momentous. Not only did she have to sneak into the living room but once she arrived there, the tunnel still needed locking and securing behind her. Storm felt sick, nausea churned in her belly. Her heart thumped violently in her chest. A pounding drummed in her ears. Breathing in gently from her nose and out through her mouth for ten seconds, she tried to calm her pulse rate down. Finn's face flashed in her mind. God only knew what he was going through. Her fear no longer mattered.

All was quiet above.

"Right let's do this." She whispered to herself.

A determined Storm raised the trapdoor, and peered into the cabin. The sound of snoring times two reverberated throughout the dimness coming from the direction of the bedroom. The sofa was empty of bodies. Squeezing through the gap she carefully opened the trapdoor fully. Hippy Claire had left a row of scented tea lights lit. She really was the most careless woman. However, the small flickering flames illuminated the cabin enough for Storm see what she was doing.

Bending down into the space, she pulled the slab back into place and locked it. The trapdoor creaked on its hinges as it closed becoming part of the rug once more. Storm glanced around her furtively. A loud coughing came from the bedroom and the sound of bedsprings and voices.

"Got any water?" The bald man said between splutters.

"Go to sleep." Hippy Claire's irritable whine.

Storm looked around in panic. Crouching behind the sofa. She saw a bulky shape head to the bathroom. Grunting and grumbling under his breath. Storm placed her hand over her mouth, barely daring to breath. The sound of running water gushed, as the bald man filled a glass, followed by a trickling noise as he peed into the toilet. Shuffling back to the bedroom, bedsprings twanged. The bald man hadn't bothered flushing the loo! Storm shook her head in disgust.

"Now that I'm awake ......" The bald guy sniggered to Hippy Claire, who giggled.

'Yuck.' Thought Storm. 'Totally gross!' She would rather get caught or fight them than listen to that. Storm shuddered. Creeping to the door she turned the key. A loud click!

"Did you hear that?" Hippy Claire said sharply.

"Not falling for that one. Wifely duties please." Sleazy murmurs and laughter filled the cabin.

Holding her breath, Storm carefully opened the door, tiptoeing quietly into the boat shed. Closing it behind her, she waited, for a minute in the shadows before taking the key to the motorboat from behind the wood slat where it was hidden. The boat had oars for short journeys or if the engine failed and

Storm slowly paddled the vessel out into the ocean. Quarter of the way out, she started the engine. The tank was full. The boat bounced happily over the waves to the quayside at Puffin Island. Collecting her rucksack, and gratefully pulling socks and boots onto her icy feet, Storm turned the boat and headed in the direction of Dunbar, keeping her speed slow and eyes alert. Fortunately, she gained visibility from the stars and the glow of a pretty crescent moon.

Checking her phone, she saw that there was still no communication from Finn. It was nearly four am and dawn would break soon. Fate decreed that she must go to Tyne Adventure Camp; but the activities that would take place, were vastly different to those listed on the itinerary. It was literally a journey into the unknown. Storm would have to dig deep and draw strength like she'd never had to before in her young life!

CHAPTER 10
Finn Locke v Adrian Dunn

In room Blue 5, Finn sat up in bed glaring at Adrian who was lying on his back in the bunk opposite. His mouth was wide open. Snore, snort, chomp, had been the regular pattern throughout the night. Finn knew this because he'd been awake every minute of it. He wondered if he could ask to transfer rooms. Room Blue 5 was painted a shabby baby blue with cracks in the paintwork. Two black steel bunkbeds with green mattresses stood in the room with one pillow and white folded linen sitting on the spare beds. Navy and white flowered curtains hung from the window over- looking a series of cabins, huts, and a football pitch, surrounded by woodland.

He glanced at his phone. It was ten past six and still only Saturday. He felt as though he'd been away from Puffin Island for weeks! A text pinged from Storm. Finn answered, venting his wrath about Adrian his room- mate. Storm seemed to be coping well, but he would phone her that evening. A week with no one to talk to, was a long time.

Finn headed to the white communal bathroom and showered. He was the only person in there. The water was hot, and the shower powerful, but the water failed to drain away, spilling out of his cubical onto the brown tiled floor. The bathroom was awash with soap suds. Turning off the water, Finn wrapped a black towel around his waist, looking around for a mop and bucket. Nothing. He would maybe ask someone. Leaving the bathroom he found the place deserted. Finn shrugged. His stomach growled with hunger.

"Morning." Adrian passed him in the corridor. Dressed in stripy pyjamas, he looked bad tempered and half asleep.

"Hiya mate." Finn replied, cheerfully. "Hey the drains blocked…!" Finn called after him. Adrian ignored him, disappearing into the bathroom.

There was a loud crash followed by a string of swear words. Adrian must have slipped over on the soapy floor. Finn grinned. There was another side to Adrian. The chummy, sanctimonious behaviour was a cover for a very different personality That was obvious. The real Adrian was already emerging. Finn threw on a dark blue track suit, white t-shirt, and black trainers, and headed down to the cafeteria. The welcome smell of cooked breakfast greeted his nostrils.

"Hiya, can I have three bacon, sausage, fried egg and do you have any potato scones, please." Finn asked, scanning the trays for them.

"Ain't got no tatty scones mate." said the Chef. "Fried bread?" He held up a greasy piece of fried bread with his mental tongs. Chef was in whites, sleeves rolled up boasting tattoos of anchors and crosses.

Finn shook his head.

"What are those?" he said pointing to crispy brown triangles stacked on the metal heated tray.

"Hash browns mate. They got potatoes in 'em."

"Cool. Five please Chef."

The chef nodded his approval.

Finn helped himself to toast, butter and tea and sat at a table by the window eating his breakfast. The hash browns were quite nice, especially dipped in egg yolk. The view looked out on an army assault course. It looked fun. He supposed that the week had parallels to basic military training but a softer fun version.

No drill practice or marching, and an array of water sports instead. Storm would love it here. If she could only get rid of the anxiety that plagued her. She was missing out on a lot of fun. Plus, she'd set her sights on joining the armed forces, but she would need a clean bill of health and the ability to stay away from home. Travel was a big part of the job. Storm was not just his cousin; she was also his best friend and he worried about her.

Adrian entered the cafeteria. Standing at five foot seven, of stocky build, his blonde hair was short and slightly greasy. He wore light grey track trousers, a sweatshirt with white trainers. Even his round-shouldered walk annoyed Finn. He was stooped and slightly cowed. He could see him glancing over.

"For goodness sake." Finn muttered under his breath. "Sit somewhere else."

Finn hoped he wasn't going to get lumbered with Adrian all week. Stiffening, he willed him to sit at another table. Adrian, however, was either not sensitive to Finn's body language, or chose to ignore it. He walked over, placing his tray down with a clatter on the cheap wooden table. His plate contained fried bread, beans, with scrambled egg. Pouring white sugar into his tea, he hesitated, obviously wanting to say something to Finn.

"Think the cleaning rota said you're on bathroom duty." He laughed nervously. His voice was soft with a high-pitched intonation. "Slipped over on the floor. All soapy and slippery." A nervous laugh again. Stirring his tea, his pale eyes failed to maintain eye contact.

"Sorry about that." Finn's deep voice rumbled, and he looked him in the eye, affording him a dark blue steely glare. "Drains blocked and couldn't find a mop." He added menacingly. "Not seen this rota, you mention?"

The 'glare' was mastered. He had copied 'the look' from one of his favourite military films. In the film, the new recruits are on basic training, and terrorised by their crazy sergeant. Sgt Moonshine would square up to them, nose to nose, giving them an evil glare whilst roaring into their faces. He derived pleasure from watching them wither and tremble! A bit sadistic but it amused Finn.

Finn had practised the evil glare, and its delivery seemed to have a similar effect on Adrian who knocked over his tea. Scraping back his chair, he scurried off to get a cloth and Finn chuckled. He fancied himself as a famous actor one day. The next Denzel Washington or the first Finn Locke!

Clearing away his tray, he went outside and walked around the island. A smaller island could be seen in the distance, about a mile out to sea. Speedboats circled periodically, leaving a white frothy trail. They looked like some kind of security detail to Finn.

First lesson of the day was in one of the huts. It was a power point presentation about sea kayaking. Then lunch, and the afternoon would be spent out on the water. Tables and chairs sat in uniformed rows and Finn sat next to a boy about his age, at the back of the room.

"Gabriel." He introduced himself to Finn. He was nice looking with dark floppy hair, dressed in jeans and a black hoody.

"Finn. Pleased to meet you mate." It was nice to see a friendly face.

The instructor flicked through the slides, asking questions to the class, in between reading out the contents.

The room was warm, and after a sleepless night Finn struggled to keep his eyes open. Gabriel nudged him and Finn awoke with a start.

"Mr Locke. Am I boring you?" The instructor was speaking to him.

Finn shook his head, aware of the sniggers from fellow students.

"No Sir. I erm didn't sleep too well. Sorry."

"Tom will do. No need for Sir." He looked at him quizzically.

"Have you kayaked before?"

"Yes, with my old man. Erm my dad." Finn rubbed his eyes.

The instructor nodded, raising his eyebrows dramatically.

"Haven't missed anything you don't already know then?" He muttered sarcastically, glancing at his watch. "Mr Locke, can I see you after class?"

Finn looked at the clock on the wall. It was twelve noon. He had literally missed half the lesson. The hut emptied rapidly, and he walked up to the instructor, towering over him in height.

"Sorry about falling asleep. Didn't mean to be rude." Finn apologised politely.

Instructor Tom scratched his head. He was a small man of five four with a receding grey hairline and brown eyes, hidden behind gold rimmed glasses. Dressed in a white shirt, black trousers, and brown shoes he looked like an accountant.

"Just what every teacher wants. Sleeping students." He said sourly. "Everything ok Mr Locke?" His accent was from North Yorkshire.

"Finn, yeah. Just the dude, the guy I'm sharing with, snored all night. Guess I'm not used to sharing. Got literally zero sleep."

Instructor Tom frowned.

"The student or dude..." He looked at his list on the clip board. "Adrian Dunn."

Finn nodded.

"That's him."

"Mr Dunn's put in a complaint about you Mr Locke. Says you covered the shower room floor in soap deliberately, so he fell and hurt his back, and when he tried to speak to you about it, you displayed aggressive and threatening behaviour towards him!"

Finn looked confused. He placed his hands behind his back and balled his fists. Adrian must have sneaked off after breakfast, to tell tales and lies about him like some pathetic kid. What a little shit!

"I couldn't find the mop. The drain was blocked. I tried to tell him. He came and sat with me at breakfast." Finn said carefully. "I may have been a bit off with him. He literally kept me awake all night snoring." He added mechanically.

"Are we going to have a problem with you Mr Locke?" Asked Tom.

Finn could feel anger surging through him. A problem with him? What on earth was going on? The evil stare had been a bad idea admittedly. He shouldn't have done it. But it was hardly threatening behaviour.

"Nah, not with me Sir. I got up, had a shower. Drain was blocked. Couldn't find the mop, so couldn't mop the floor. I ate my breakfast and came to class."

"You seem a little hostile Mr Locke." Tom raised his eyebrows. "Not sure what it's like where you're from but here, we are nice people!"

"No, not at all." Finn attempted to break the tension by laughing. "Nah not hostile. Just don't get it. Is this like for real? What do you mean where I come from?" Was Tom referring to Scotland?

"It's maybe, not such a nice place as here." Tom continued. "I'm wondering. Hence your attitude."

"Because I'm black! That's it. Isn't it!" Finn was speechless. "Is that what you meant? I must come from a rough place because I'm black! To set you straight, I don't. I live in an amazing place as it happens." His voice sounded strained and controlled. He pasted a grin onto his face. He was boiling with rage but attempting to cover it. Tom's accusations were false and with prejudice.

Perhaps they would send him home. He wished he'd never come. He'd genuinely had a bad feeling about the trip to Tyne Adventures but had attributed this to his anxiety over Storm staying alone on Puffin Island. Perhaps there was more to it. Sneaky Adrian clearly had it in for him and was playing the good-natured helpful victim, painting Finn as an aggressive loose cannon who was bullying him.

"No, I did not mean that lad. I'm no racist. You're paranoid, putting words into my mouth that I have not uttered. Maybe smooth it over with Adrian, is all I'm saying. An apology never cost anyone anything." He gave Finn an intense stare of dislike. "Adrian's actually my step-son and he's a good lad. Can't see him making things up." His smile failed to reach his cold eyes.

Finn opened his mouth to argue that he had nothing to apologise for; but the final comment had closed the door on the conversation. Finn decided to play it cool.

"I'll do that." Finn said calmly. "I'll speak to him." Turning he left the hut. He felt like punching a wall to rubble. Pity boxing wasn't next on the schedule. He could pretend the bag was Adrian's smug face.

If this madness continued with Instructor Tom and his pathetic stepson Adrian, he would just leave Tyne Island and head home. He'd pay his mother back the money for the camp. At fifteen Finn was self-aware. Yes, he had faults, but he saw himself as a good-natured fair person and was not willing to put up with manipulation, lies or mind games from anyone, especially not the likes of Adrian Dunn and his stepdad!

He texted Storm, mentioning only that the morning had been boring. No point adding to her anxiety at this stage. He'd call her that evening. Maybe by then things would have calmed down or he would be on his way back to Scotland. The thought of Puffin Island, Storm, swimming, diving, and exploring the Emerald Pool Chamber, and the Creepy Cave, seemed like heaven.

Entering the cafeteria, he chose broccoli and stilton soup with a beef and mustard roll. Filling a large mug with coffee. He spied Adrian sitting eating sausages and beans over by the window where they'd sat at breakfast. He smiled at a couple of the other students and walked over to Adrian. Sitting down opposite him. He dipped his beef roll into the soup. It was delicious.

"Enjoy the lecture?" he asked Adrian.

Adrian shifted uncomfortably in his seat.

"Was ok." His eyes were cast down as if counting baked beans.

"Seems you have a problem with me Aidie."

"Oh!" Adrian cut up his sausage. "I do. Do I?" His tone was surly.

Finn nodded, mopping up the remainder of his soup with the roll. He chewed, looking Adrian straight in the eyes.

"You don't know me. I'm a down to earth guy. What you see is what you get. I'm not gonna be sneaking around, soaping floors, so people I've just met slip over and hurt themselves. I'm not the type of guy who enjoys being passive aggressive for kicks. Saying one thing and meaning another. If you piss me off, you'll know about it. Tom the instructor, er... your stepdad, says I frightened you and you thought I was trying to hurt you. That was not my intention. I apologise."

Adrian stared at Finn's empty soup bowl. A pink colour rose in his pale cheeks.

"I know about you." he muttered. Scraping his chair back, he picked up his tray. Looking down at Finn, he smiled. "You wait." he said quietly and scuttled off laughing.

Finn looked at his disappearing figure in bewilderment. The feeling of unease tightened in his belly. What on earth did that mean? I know about you. You wait!

Leaving the cafeteria Finn had half an hour to spare before they headed out to sea in Kayaks. They'd been instructed to leave all phones in their rooms in case they capsized. Finn wrapped his in a couple of freezer bags along with his cash and put it in the zipped up inside pocket of his thick black hoody. He didn't trust Adrian not to steal or snoop or take it just to cause him trouble. He changed into a fresh black t-shirt, track trousers, hoody and trainers. He tidied his sleeping area. He'd brought the minimum kit with him and his rucksack contained only his charger, a change of clothes and toiletries.

Outside he joined some of the other boys on the army assault course. Finn, tall and athletic excelled, battling only with one other boy, Gabriel who he'd sat next to in the hut earlier that day. They shook hands good naturedly after Finn beat him to the finish line. It was a bright and sunny day, and the cobalt blue sky was dotted with smatterings of wispy white cloud. The ocean glinted a dark green. Seagulls shrieked and the light breeze wafted sea salt inland.

The two o'clock Kayak lesson arrived. Tom the instructor from earlier was taking the class. Finn's heart sank! Dressed in navy gym clothes he handed out life jackets, bellowing instructions about safety, and the importance of following his orders. He handed Finn a grey one. Finn was surprise that Tom hadn't punctured it.

Finn strapped it on and sat in the Kayak following instructions.

They were in the harbour area which was like a giant paddling pool. The stone harbour wall left a gap of about twenty metres to enable access for fishing trawlers and other boats. There was a motorboat out to the right in the bay, near the small island. Finn decided to ask Gabriel about it.

Paddling up to him he asked:

"What's with the patrols on that wee island?"

"Some oil refinery, but not sure what else is on there to warrant all that. Fenton Island it's called."

"Seems a lot of security."

Gabriel nodded.

"Yeah, I thought same."

"Concentrate Mr Locke. I know you think you're better than everyone else, but there's some here, new to this!" Tom bellowed angrily at him. "They want to learn and improve."

"Sorry." Finn whispered to Gabriel, glaring at Tom. "Don't want to get you into trouble."

"He's an idiot. You're alright." Gabriel muttered under his breath. "He's a rubbish instructor. He's got it in for you. Best ignore him." Gabriel appraised Tom through narrowed eyes. His accent was English and well spoken. Gabriel had a natural air of confidence about him.

"And now corrupting Mr Sharp, are you Mr Locke?" Tom shouted across the water.

"That's hardly fair." Gabriel called back crossly. "Leave the fellow alone." He scowled, adding to Finn. "Man's a bloody bully."

Tom went purple with rage.

"You are on a warning Mr Locke! Inciting mutiny!"

"Thanks mate. But leave it. He's got a problem with me." Finn said quietly to Gabriel.

Finn paddled away moving further out to the sea entrance. The instructor was clearly unhinged. He was done with Tyne Adventures. His mother had paid substantial money for him to attend and have fun, not to be singled out and humiliated by the instructor. He was out of there! After the lesson he would grab his bag and get on the first train back to Scotland. The decision was made.

Instructor Tom zoomed up alongside him in the yellow instructor kayak.

"You are going to have an advanced lesson with one of our senior instructors. You're obviously way ahead of everyone else." He called loudly for all the class to hear. "You'll be back later than the rest. However, I think you'll enjoy. Seems we got off to a bad start, that's all. Follow me Mr Locke."

Pulling a confused face, Finn paddled out into the dark emerald sea following Tom. The sea was calm with mere ripples for waves. Picking up speed they whizzed past the harbour walls and out into the vast ocean. The wind immediately became stronger pushing Finn forward.

Heading to the right, Finn glanced back. Obscured by the grey harbour wall, he could no longer see the rest of the class. They were heading towards Fenton Island, and as they neared ,Finn could see that it consisted of a mass of dense green forest, sandy beaches, and a small quay.

Tom paddled in the direction of a motorboat that had been patrolling earlier. It had ventured in nearer to Tyne Island, bobbing on the water, a few meters away. Two men in khaki sat watching them. They wore black sunglasses, and were bald, and of a heavy build. Finn's stomach churned with anxiety. Something was seriously wrong, there was no way they were senior kayak instructors!

Turning his Kayak, he began paddling back to Tyne Island. Going against the tide was hard work. Images flashed through his mind of the gangsters landing on Puffin Island back in May. Were the men in the motorboat, gang members intent on revenge? Every ounce of strength went into his strokes, but the wind and pull of the waves went against him. His mind screamed DANGER! Finn knew he was finished. He was a blood-soaked man floating in a warm sea filled with hungry sharks!

"Locke get back here now!" The instructor screamed at him.

The motorboat engine started up causing a large swell. Finn could feel the kayak swaying unsteadily, threatening to capsize. The next minute the motorboat zoomed in front of him cutting the engine. The men were shouting at Instructor Tom to pull the string at the back of the kayak. Tom did so, towing him to the motorboat. Grabbing hands pulled Finn out of the kayak by his life jacket. Before he could struggle, a stinking cloth covered his mouth and nose. His head felt fuzzy and then blackness.

CHAPTER 11
Storm v Anxiety

Arriving near Dunbar harbour, Storm debated whether to head further down the coastline. The train journey was daunting, and she wished to avoid it as much as possible. Anxiety began to pulse. Storm felt lightheaded. Her chest ached, and her legs felt heavy. Her heart was racing. Slowing the boat, Storm practised her breathing exercises once more. She took a small breath in through her nose, and then exhaled longer breaths out through her mouth. Holding her pulse, she persevered until she felt the thudding beats slow and her head clear. Her body relaxed and the aches subsided. Storm smiled, shaking her head in disbelief. It was like a miracle for her. This was the second time that day this method had worked. Finally, Storm knew how to control her anxiety instead of it controlling her. Through her breathing she could stop anxiety from starting its ugly ritual of possession. This discovery was mind blowing and a massive breakthrough for her.

The train ride will be ok, she told herself. Finn needed her. Motoring into the harbour Storm parked the boat along the quayside. Locking and securing it, she grabbed her rucksack. Grandad Flint had a permit to moor the boat there as he often travelled down the coast by sea when heading into town or down to England. It was a relaxing alternative to road travel.

Storm waved back at some young fishermen heading out for the morning catch. Dressed in overalls they grinned at her as they passed, glancing back admiringly. It must be the makeup, Storm thought. It made her feel a bit weird. She wasn't sure she liked the sensation or the attention.

"Stop over- thinking." Storm whispered to the chatter in her brain.

Over-thinking was the loyal companion to anxiety, it included over analysing and being too intense about situations, however simple they were. That was another area that she needed to work on. Storm grinned. This new self-awareness was pretty cool. Finn would be so impressed!

Dunbar Station loomed in the distance. The first train was in half an hour at six am. Hippy Clare and her bald husband would be so confused to find that this time, the motorboat had vanished in the night. The smaller boat that Storm had set adrift had been found and returned by Coastguard to the boat house, undamaged and so Hippy Clare still had transport to Puffin Island. Storm was worried about Marmite and Marmalade. She had left an oval window in the hallway open for them. It was large enough for them to jump in and out but not big enough for an intruder to squeeze through. The cats were hunters and so if neglected or abandoned by Hippy Clare, could live off mice if they had to.

Perched on a chocolate brown bench at Dunbar station, Storm ate a couple of the chicken mayonnaise sandwiches she'd prepared earlier. They were scrumptious! Checking her phone, she saw that there was still nothing from Finn. The locations told her he was still at Tyne Adventures. Suddenly his emoji pinged and moved out to sea. Storm frowned, startled by the sudden movement! Was it a glitch caused by bad mobile reception or was Finn on the move? Storm was certain that Finn was in trouble. Radio Silence had been well over twelve hours.

The announcement for the arrival of the London Euston train echoed over the tannoy system. Storm took a breath, as the long grey and red train wound its way into the station. The journey to London Euston was uneventful. Storm, like Finn previously, ate most of the way to London, reasoning that the sandwiches would go off. Plus, it broke up the boredom of the long journey. Reaching Euston Station, she was overwhelmed by how busy it was. People of all ages were rushing about, some in smart business dress, students, tourists, and travellers like herself. Traffic glinted in long rows with engines roaring, horns beeping, the drone of helicopters hovering and distant police sirens blaring. The cloudy air was thicker and warmer, laced with fumes. Storm's nose wrinkled. After the pure air and peace of Puffin Island, it was like entering a new noisy world.

After checking the map of the tube station, Storm made her way to the taxi rank.

"Like no way." Storm shook her head.

The appearance of the underground station, for her was terrifying, with thousands of people buzzing around like worker bees in a hive. The map of the tube lines: Northern, Jubilee, Bakerloo to name a few, with the colour codes and zigzag map lines, was too confusing for Storm. It was like reading a foreign language that she'd never learned. Sitting back in the black taxi she breathed a temporary sigh of relief.

Waterloo Station was equally hectic. Purchasing a ticket from the vending machine. Storm weaved her way to Platform 11 where the train was waiting to leave for Poole in Dorset. This part of the journey would take about two hours and twenty minutes. Estimated time of arrival was approximately one forty-five. The train creaked and squealed as it pulled off. Crossing the River Thames, the Houses of Parliament glowed a honey brown in the sunlight. It was an elegant building pivotal to the life force of the energetic capital. Vast yachts and cruisers sat on the water of the Thames. The London Eye loomed. Storm could see people sitting at the top. It was so high!

"Any snacks! Hot drinks!" A smart lady dressed in a red uniform clattered along the narrow isle pushing a food trolley packed with crisps, peanuts, cookies, and miniature bottles of alcohol.

Storm bought a hot chocolate. It tasted sweet and comforting and reminded her of Puffin Island. Consuming homemade cheese and onion pasties, and bacon flavoured crisps, Storm contemplated the next aspect of the journey. The plan formulated was flexible. In other words, Storm had no idea what she would discover at Tyne Island and would have to think on her feet from now on.

Checking the map app on her phone, Poole station appeared to be quite a distance from the quayside. In addition, she would need to travel by boat over to Tyne Island. Leaving the train at Poole, Storm walked through the station. It was small and quiet with numerous white taxis waiting outside. Again, Storm felt gratitude for the money she had. It made life a lot easier. Passing a maze of built- up residential streets, industrial areas, and Parks on the way, they eventually arrived at Poole Harbour Quayside. The water was crowded with a variety of moored vessels, from fishing boats to tour cruisers. Their masts clanged and jangled in the breeze, like percussion instruments.

"You off to camp Miss. Dropped some kids off yesterday." The taxi driver was dark skinned, plump and friendly with a shock of white hair and twinkly brown eyes.

"I missed the train, so am in a bit of trouble. Should have come yesterday!" Storm replied to the taxi driver. "Need to get over to the Island but the camp boats gone."

The Taxis driver nodded, chuckling.

"Me mates got a tour boat. He can ferry you over. I'll call 'im for ya if you like." He said. "Got a daughter your age, she's late for everything and is always gettin' into bover too. Calmed down now a bit though and at Uni." He added proudly.

"Oh cool." Said Storm pleased that she looked older. "What's she studying?"

"Psychology." He nodded. "What 'bout you?"

"Not sure. Armed Forces I think."

The taxi driver nodded in acknowledgement. Storm shouldn't be chatting to him like this. She was supposed to be anonymous but already she could imagine the taxi driver telling his wife over fish and chips and a pint about the young girl he'd picked up in his taxi that day.

"Yeah, if you could call your mate. That'd be great. Thanks very much." Storm smiled.

"You not from here." The taxi driver was referring to her Scottish accent.

"Highlands." Storm lied. Well compared to Dorset, Puffin Island might as well be in the Highlands and she had spent quite a bit of time on Shetland in the past, so not a complete lie.

The Taxis driver phoned his friend and took her further down a bumpy road to where 'Queen of Poole' was moored.

"Look after 'ere Bill. She's come from the Highlands, same age as my Kaitlin." The taxi driver bellowed to his friend as he dropped her off.

Bill was short and had tattoos down his forearms of blue anchors and ships. With sun kissed skin, sandy hair and very blue eyes, he told Storm that he used to be in the Navy.

"Do you ever hire out the boat?" Storm asked as they zoomed across the green water towards the island.

"Time to time." He nodded, dropping her off at the quay. Storm noticed several rowing and motorboats moored there.

"Please let me pay you?" Storm offered.

"Nah." He gave her a scrutinising look. "Sure you're ok miss? I got good instincts like, and you look awful young to be traipsing around on your tod. You ain't eighteen are ya? Don't worry I won't say nuffing."

He held out his business card.

"In case you get in bother. Shout me."

Storm smiled and took it from him.

"I'm good. Really. But thanks." She avoided the age question.

"As I say, you get in trouble, shout me!" He glanced at her boots, obviously recognising them and the rucksack as military issue. The boots had been issued at Air Cadets and the rucksack was one of her dads. "Can't kid a kidder."

"Thanks." said Storm. "If I get in trouble I will." If only, she wished. It would be a relief to share the burden of her mission. But to share even with a friend, was one person too many.

He nodded and shot back over to the mainland leaving behind a churning line of white froth.

Storm looked around her. The original booking confirmation email from Tyne Adventures was on her phone. If stopped by staff she could show it. However, she was in the heart of enemy camp. Storm had no idea yet of the dangers that lurked within. Thick forests lay to the left of her. Carefully she moved into the dense green undergrowth, needing to decide her next course of action.

So much for stealth. The taxi driver, and his navy friend knew she was from Scotland and if there was CCTV she'd have been seen arriving on the island. In a way, because her arrival was so clumsy and obvious, it may not raise suspicion. However, Storm needed to step up her game and switch to battle mode from now on, or she would blow the whole operation. Think strategically, she told herself and be confident.

Storm emerged from the woods and sauntered along the path that led from the quayside up to the cabins, huts and outbuildings sprawled out ahead. There was an old guardhouse at the entrance to Tyne Adventure Camp. But no sign of it being manned. Storm passed through the raised barrier. There were sign posts for male and female accommodation. Pulling up her hood she tightened the drawstring and made her way to the 'Blue' block. Her heart hammered in her chest. There were a few young people milling about, but most she supposed would be involved in activities.

Arriving at a rundown building, near the football pitch, she pushed the pale blue door of the male accommodation. It was locked! Walking around the side of the building, a window that led into a bathroom, had been left open. Storm climbed in without effort. The rooms were numbered. Blue 5 Locke and Dunn was up the corridor on the left. Nudging it with her foot, the door swung open. The room was empty and sparse. Storm spotted Finn's rucksack by his bed. Rushing to it she searched frantically for clues, but it contained only clothes, a phone charger, and toiletries. His phone was missing.

The bunk of Adrian Dunn had been vacated. There was no luggage just a discarded white sheet and a pillow on the bed. Storm visibly jumped as it occurred to her that Dunn was the same surname as the Senior Administrator, Rude Jane Dunn, the sister of Hippy Clare. Literally, the ugly sisters. Adrian Dunn must be her son. Ice ran through Storm. There was a plot in play, for certain! Unanswered questions demanded answers. Storm began to shake. Finn had been kidnapped; she was sure of it!

Clarity shone brightly. Finn's disappearance was the work of the gangsters whose fellow members had perished near Puffin Island earlier that year. Josh, Finn's dad had infiltrated the gang and snatched vast quantities of money from right under their nose. What if Finn had been taken as a trade-off to be exchanged for the return of the money. The gang members were ruthless. They may not plan to release Finn at all, blaming the Locke and Swift family for the loss of life of their friends and for taking the money. Finn's life was in danger that was without a doubt!

Would the police take her seriously if she called them, she wondered? She had no proof apart from Finn's radio silence and the conversations she'd overheard. But then she would have to divulge how she'd heard them; subsequently disclosing information regarding the tunnels and the underground world. The secrets of Puffin Island had to be maintained no matter what. Difficult questions would be asked about why she'd stayed hidden on Puffin Island instead of attending camp and the fraudulent email. No, the Police were not an option.

Her dad was the person to call. She tried his mobile. A message told her 'This mobile may be switched off'. Storm sighed with irritation.

The phone reception bars displayed: 'no signal'. Attempting to call her mother and Grandad Flint, the phone refused to ring. The mobile signal was diabolical on the island and kept dipping. Storm reasoned that If Finn could have text or phoned her, he would have. If she called him, and his phone rang, she could endanger him further. His hoody was padded and there was a secret pocket underneath the actual pocket. He may have his phone hidden. If it was confiscated, she would no longer have any means of tracking him.

Storm was alone.

Zooming in on Finn's last movement, she saw that he was in fact on a small island next to Tyne Island called Fenton Isle. The island was tiny and a mere spec. At a glance it appeared that he was out to sea and a location glitch. Fenton Isle was approximately a mile to the right. One of the rowing boats at the quay would be sufficient to reach it. The sandy beaches surrounding Tyne Island had an inner circle of thick lush green woodland that would hide her movements. Storm headed to the shelter of the trees, creeping cautiously around to the far side of the island where she had a clear view of Fenton Isle. An ancient grey oak tree stood by a gurgling stream. Water ran down through the woods into a gully in the yellow sand, flowing out to the sea. The tree had a thick stubbly trunk where old branches had snapped off. It was the perfect hiding place. Climbing upwards she reached a natural seat halfway up. Placing the rucksack to the side of her, Storm pulled her phone from her pocket. The plan was to stay hidden until twilight and then sneak over to the island and try to locate Finn.

One bar showed. Finally! Checking Finn's location, she saw he was still where she'd last seen him. No movement or messages. Storm decided to text her parents and Grandad Flint before calling them in case reception dipped and the call was cut off. Then at least they would be alerted to the situation. Pins and needles shot down her leg from sitting in the same position on the hard rough wood. Storm shifted her body, to the left, freeing a small fresh branch trapped beneath her. It pinged back like elastic, knocking the phone from her hand.

Storm screamed as it fell crashing into the stream below. The back of the phone severed on impact. It lay in two pieces in the cold murky brown water! Scrambling down the tree like monkey, she grabbed it. The screen was cracked. Voices sounded in the distance and Storm hastily returned to the safety of the oak tree, bashing, and bruising her knees and shins in haste. Rubbing the wet damaged phone on her hoody she managed to clip the back on. Switching the phone back on, nothing happened. A black screen! The phone was dead! Maybe it needed to dry out and wasn't completely broken; but for now, Storm had no method of communication. Even if she reached an old operational telephone box, they'd used in the olden days to make phone calls, she had no knowledge of phone numbers. All the information was on her smashed 'phone!

Storm felt like crying. Finn was in danger and missing! He might even be dead. She was miles away from home, with no way of contacting her parents. The mission ahead now seemed impossible! To add stress to the situation, the voices she'd heard were nearing and she was dying to go to the toilet! Plus, she should never have screamed, she may have alerted them. It had just been such a shock seeing her phone drop and smash. Tears rolled down her face and she wiped them away with her sleeve. This was not the time to weaken. Tonight, she would head over to the tiny island, find Finn and they would travel back together to Puffin Island where they'd sit in the Emerald Pool Chamber and laugh about yet another adventure. Storm had to stay focussed and positive. Shaking off misery, she made a plan.

CHAPTER 12
A Grim Situation

Finn awoke. He was lying on cold concrete in complete darkness. The smell of oil mixed with sea salt wafted around him. Machinery hummed nearby. He was inside some kind of building. Trying to accustom his eyes to the dark, shapes slowly began to form. Shady images. A crack of light like an upside down 'L' must be a door. A locked door has hinges. The hinges were the weakest point. If he could free himself from his restraints, he'd have a chance. His hands were taped behind his back and his legs, knees and feet had also been tied together. Finn was a tall, muscular build for his age and whoever had taken him was aware of this.

Lifting his legs, he bent his knees bringing them into his chest. This enabled him to slip his arms through his legs to the front. Finn was fully clothed. For that he was thankful. The thick hoody had a strong zip. His Dad had bought it for him shortly before he went missing the first time. It had been expensive. The zip was half down. If he rubbed the tape up and down, the zip would work as a blunt knife and fray and cut it away. Sitting up he began rubbing the tape up and down the jagged teeth.

This whole trip to Tyne Adventure Camp had been masterminded. Adrian Dunn was part of the conspiracy. Finn had known from the first meeting that there was no way Adrian was fifteen. If he got his hands on him he'd beat him to pulp, and the evil Instructor Tom. Yet those two were probably just the small players. He was sure it was connected to the money his father Josh had stolen from the counterfeit money gang during the undercover operation.

The stink of the substance they'd placed over his mouth and nose clung to the hairs on his nostrils causing nausea. Leaning over Finn was sick. Thankfully they hadn't taped his mouth, or he would have choked to death on his own vomit. He could feel a weight on his left side. His phone must still be hidden in the secret pocket. He knew that Storm would be worried sick by now. Help would be on its way. He just hoped it got there in time!

He needed some water desperately. Heavy footsteps approached. There was a fumbling noise outside and the door burst open. Brilliant sunlight flooded the place of confinement and Finn was temporarily blinded by the light. A tall stocky silhouette framed the doorway and a man walked in dressed in khaki wearing a balaclava and black boots. The illumination showed that Finn was lying in a small empty grey stone room. There were windows at the top of the internal wall and a red door led further into the building. It had a padlock hanging from it and a white sign with red writing that read: 'NO ENTRY TO UNAUTHORISED PERSONNEL. WATER TREATMENT PLANT'.

The man bent down seizing a hunting knife from the black holster strapped to his leg. A gleaming blade of silver sliced through the tape that bound Finn's wrists. Balaclava handed him a bottle of water. Noting the pile of vomit, he shook his head handing Finn a mars bar. Finn was starving but eyed the bar suspiciously. Opening the bottle, he drank the entire contents. His body immediately felt energised.

"The chocolate ain't poisoned." Balaclava said. He had a southern English accent. "You, ok?" nodding at the sick.

Finn shook his head.

"Nah, not really. Why am I here?" he asked quietly.

Assessing the enemy, Finn was bigger and stronger and could physically over-power the man. However, this was not taking into account skill sets. The proficient way Balaclava handled the hunting knife had stopped Finn from attempting to knock him over and run. The knife with the powerful curved jagged blade was a lethal weapon and Balaclava obviously knew how to use it. Finn did not want to end up sliced and diced. He was fifteen and had a life to lead.

The man opened the mars bar wrapper and broke off a piece and ate it to prove it wasn't laced with poison. Handing the bar back, Finn who devoured it.

"Why am I here?" He repeated.

"Ask your old man." Balaclava said standing up straight.

"Dunno where he is. Honestly. I haven't seen or heard from him in over a year." He looked Balaclava in the eyes.

"Yeah 'Es good at disappearing that one. That's why you're here. Flush 'im out."

"It won't work. Have no clue where he is. No one does. He won't even know I'm here."

"'E'll know."

"This is messed up." Finn said desperately. "I don't want this shit."

If he ever got out of there alive, he swore he was going to live under Puffin Island for the rest of his life!

"Well, you got it. Thank the old man. 'E don't seem to 'ave your welfare at heart does 'e." The balaclava crouched down and wound tape around his wrists again. "While we're 'aving a chat. That cousin of yours. Where is she?"

Finn tensed. Damn, his body language had given away his weakness.

He shook his head.

"Was supposed to be coming. Changed her mind." Finn said slowly.

"But where is she?" Balaclava's tone was menacing.

Finn had only one card to play. Honest ignorance.

"Stayed at home. Her Mum's friend is house sitting and Storm said she wanted to stay on the island." His story was feasible.

"You expect me to believe…? Why she stay at home?"

The man smelt of stale cigarettes.

"She has mental health problems, anxiety, and can't cope with this sort of thing, like adventure camp!" Finn spoke honestly.

"Swift's girl has mental health problems!" The man roared with laughter. "This gets better. Jez what an admission! Now I know you're not making it up!"

"Glad you find it funny." What an absolute dick! Finn could feel anger and hatred surging through him. He had to appear calm.

"'Mind your mouth." he snapped. "'Er Mum's friend. 'Er name?"

"It's Clare. Dunno her other name. Just call her Hippy Clare." Finn spoke precisely. He was controlling his rage and stopping his body from shaking as adrenalin surged. It was hard work.

Balaclava snorted with laughter.

"Hippy Clare!"

"I swear. Storm, she saw me off on the train, then went back to the island. On my life." Finn nodded.

He was telling the truth. It was a matter of life and death, and his captor would know if he was lying. He would simply miss out anything that would help the gang succeed in their quest. Storm would either be safe underground on Puffin Island, or hopefully on her way down south to rescue him. They would never find her.

"Bit economical with the truth, is she - your cousin?" asked Balaclava.

"Can be…" Finn said seriously. If he kicked his legs out from under him……? The scenario played out in his mind, but the hunting knife was always the winner.

"Problem we 'ave is that there was s'posed to be the two of you 'ere in this 'ere treatment plant. But your cuz 'as gone an' done one. Gone AWOL!" He paced up and down. "Hippy Clare as you call the dumb cow. Now 'er husband was guarding Puffin Island and he ain't seen 'er. Dumb Hippy Clare is house sitting, as you say but she ain't laid eyes on 'er. Clare's sister Jane, is the admin at the camp, an' on our pay." Balaclava lit a cigarette. " 'er and her husband Tom are both on our pay, and paid a lot of money to make sure things went smoothly an' both you an' cousin Storm was 'ere, booked in for a week at adventure camp. Until a last-minute cancellation email. "

"So, you knew she wasn't coming then. Storm I mean." Finn was genuinely confused.

"Nah Jane failed to divulge the email. Scared she wasn't gonna get paid. Thought she could lie her way out of it by saying your cuz just hadn't turned up to buy time. Thought she could con us."

"How?"

"I ask the questions!" he growled. "She cooked up the idea of distracting you by causing bother between you an' Adrian 'er son...so it was easy picking you up in the kayak cos your mind was elsewhere. Her sis and hubby in the meanwhile were frantically searching for Storm. The plan was they brought 'er here asap. Problem is they can't find 'er and they got found out. Don't worry Jane the admin will pay for her mistake!" He glanced at his watch. "Will be paying as we speak, make her even uglier, if that's even possible. Where's your phone?"

The water and mars bar churned around Finn's belly.

"In my rucksack in the room back at camp." Finn said casually. "Weren't allowed to take it. Instructor Tom said in case the kayak capsized." Despite his prowess for acting his words echoed empty and insincere.

"Hmmm. Lots of things disappearing around the Dunns'. Little shit may 'ave 'ad it. Nicked it."

"Great." Finn looked genuinely annoyed.

"From what you say. It ties in. But my bruver John was killed at Puffin Island." Balaclava said. "And my mate Sid blown to pieces on the Yacht!"

Finn shook his head in horror. He was doomed.

"We had nothing to do with that I swear. The weather that night was grim! You've no clue. It was wild, no one could've survived in that sea. No one killed him and the Yacht was a fuel leak."

"That's what they told you." He shook his head blowing out a cloud of toxic smoke. "Captain Locke and Swift are gonna pay. We want our money back an' your gonna help us get it. Question is where is your cuz Storm?"

"I swear I don't know." Finn shook his head frantically. "I would not muck you about. I'm not an idiot. I can see you're a serious guy. Are you gonna kill me?"

Balaclava looked him in the eye. Silence reigned. Chucking the cigarette onto the floor he ground it with his boot.

"Be back later. You're being moved." He said eventually. "You better 'ave a good think where she is or I won't be being so nice next visit. Got it.?"

Finn nodded. The situation was dark. The fact he'd been mainly honest with his interrogator had been in his favour as Balaclava obviously had a built-in bullshit detector. Truth was he didn't know where Storm was. They were both in serious trouble.

Balaclava headed for the door. Suddenly he stopped and turned around. Kneeling next to Finn he began a search of his clothing. Finn unintentionally held his breath. The man stank of fags and beer. He knelt back on his heels for a moment and then went through the inside of Finn's jacket. Fingers probing in the inside pocket. The secret pocket had a zip. Balaclava's fingers found it.

"See I used to be a military copper, many moons ago. Trained in searching little shits who lie. You was doing so well."

He pulled back the zip and removed the phone.

" 'Course I lied about the phone." Finn said morosely. "I'm fifteen and I don't want to die. Sorry I lied but the rest of what I said is true."

"Oh, I know what you lied about. I'm not daft. Why do you think I stopped and searched you?" He threw the phone on the floor and stamped on it repeatedly until fragments of the inwards were scattered over the stone floor. "Useless Adrian was s'posed to have searched ya."

Bending down he grabbed Finn by the scruff of the neck, punching him in the face.

Finn cried out in pain. He could feel pin pricks of heat rush to his cheek.

"Just a light punishment. Lie again it'll be worse for ya. You ain't getting no food now neither."

Balaclava left, locking the door behind him, plunging Finn into darkness once more.

Finn was imprisoned and powerless. Imminent death sat next to him in his cold dreary cell. Storm was out in the world, unaware that she was being hunted by ruthless gangsters. Alone they were weak. They needed to join forces; face the gang and situation together. Finn had to act fast. He willed Storm to be careful but to come to Fenton Isle and help him. Rubbing the tape furiously on the zip, there was enough friction to cause a fire. SNAP! The tape broke and Finn's hands were freed.

CHAPTER 13

Progress

Storm held her breath. Down below her, standing on the leaf strewn forest floor were a group of men. They were bald and dressed in khaki with black boots. Praying they wouldn't look up, she tried to merge into the tree hiding her face behind a thick branch.

Sitting down on a fallen log, the men stopped for a smoke.

"He don't know where the girl Storm is. 'Es not a bad lad. Shame." said Balaclava. "Gutsy for fifteen and got sense."

"'E lied about the phone." His colleague pointed out. He had a Welsh accent.

"Yeah, but that was transparent. The rest 'e was co-operating. Punished him!"

"Oh yeah?" Welsh nodded his approval.

"Smashed the phone into little pieces and punched him one." Balaclava said. "But if 'e don't know. Then where the hell is she?"

Storm felt sick.

"If she ain't on Puffin Island?" Welsh sounded frustrated. "She ain't here! One fourteen-year-old causing a massive headache!"

Balaclava shook his head.

"Gawd knows. Needle in a bleeding haystack. Vanished like a puff of smoke. Bit of a handful that one. 'E says she's got mental problems."

"Swift's girl?" Welsh sounded surprised.

"Yeah. That the reason for not coming."

"Perhaps she's gotta fella?"

"Dunno. We need to find 'er." Balaclava scratched his head. "Been a massive cock up. You dealt with the Dunn's? Was hoping to move fast. Delay is shit. Swift will get wind soon, then all hell with break loose."

"Dunns dealt with, yeah. Taught them a lesson an' no cash. We movin' the boy tonight?"

"Nah 'ave to be the morning now first light. I've gotta meet with the boss. She is not a happy lady. The Dunn's won't talk?"

"They're shit scared." One of the other men spoke. He had a quiet Kent accent. "They talk, they're dead, an' they knows we ain't messing about!"

Balaclava laughed.

"No, we ain't. Not one bit. Least I can rely on you three. Eyes peeled in case she turns up looking for 'im."

The four men walked off in the direction they'd come.

Storm sat absorbing the conversation. It was ironic that the gang were so desperate to find her, yet she was right next to them, sitting up a tree!

Her plan needed changing. If the gang were hunting her, it would be dangerous and stupid to beam shafts of torchlight about the woods at night. But there was no way she could return to the quay in pitch blackness. She would have to go now and hide out near the rowing boat. But there were half hourly sea patrols. The mission was thwart with danger. Storm pondered whether to use the diving equipment, but would ninety minutes of air be enough to get there and back? She watched a variety of boats dotted out on the water; laughter filled the air as the students took their sailing class.

Storm was at a loss. She had no idea what to do. Maybe if she mingled in with the class, she'd be less conspicuous. There were a few fishing boats out on the bay too. Pulling her woollen hat on to cover her dark emerald hair, she tucked in her plait. She checked her phone. It was still dead. Scrambling down the tree, she covered any tracks before going to the toilet behind a bush.

The best idea was to follow the line of the beach around to the quayside. Storm traipsed along the edge of the woods enjoying the light breeze. The sun shone glistening spotlights through thousands of treetops, illuminating moss and leaves that were changing to an autumnal gold, red, rust, burgundy and orange. Every nerve in her body was on high alert. Would she ever see Finn or Puffin Island again? Shutting the voices of uncertainty down, she began to jog, dodging fallen branches and muddy puddles. Arriving at the quay, Storm saw masses of teenagers milling about dressed in life jackets, yoga pants, trainers and hoody's, similar clothes to herself. What a turn of fortune.

Groups of chattering girls were getting into rowing boats and heading out into the bay. She heard one pretty girl with long blonde hair mentioning a 'free period'. Storm looked like just another student. She couldn't have wished for better camouflage. Climbing into a rowing boat called 'Popeye', she followed the others out into the sea. A couple of instructors were monitoring them, ready to assist in case they got into difficulty. A few of the smaller boats were heading to Fenton Isle which was out of bounds. Storm rowed furiously, keeping up with them but she drifted over to the right slightly away from them. They all landed on the island at the same time. However, the teenagers parked their boat up the beach onto the sand, whilst Storm pulled hers up into the surrounding woodland. Taking a branch, she raked away her tracks before covering the boat with masses of foliage.

Hiding by the boat she saw a patrol speed boat whizzing past and angry voices shouting as 'security' challenged the teenagers for embarking on an illegal beach. The teenagers laughed and swore at them. A heated arguement commenced. Storm grinned. She had successfully arrived on the small island, thanks to them. The next challenge was to locate Finn.

CHAPTER 14
Hinges and Hugs

Finn felt carefully along the chilly stone floor, fishing out a piece of glass from his destroyed phone. Sawing the tape, he freed his legs from the binds. He slowly stood up. His body was stiff from being tied and lying on the cold ground. Feeling around the crack of light he came to the hinges. They were old and the wooden frame was starting to rot. Going back to the phone he took a flat piece of the motherboard and attempted to move the screws. His fingers closed on his sim card. He dropped it into his inside pocket.

Removing the screws with the metal was an impossible task. If he booted the door, he'd alert any guards on the island. For all he knew there could be one standing outside the door. Taking the piece of glass, he began to dig out the wood around the hinges. It was a hard job but even if it weakened them enough to pull the door off Finn was determined to persevere. The alternative was death. Balaclavas steely look and silence had confirmed their intention.

Finn sucked his finger. He had succeeded only in cutting himself. Digging at the wood he was frustrated to find it was only rotten on the surface. The sound of metal against metal tapping on the other side of the door, caused Finn to freeze. He stopped what he was doing and moved back dropping the glass with a clink onto the floor. What on earth was it. The noise went on for ages. Finn stepped back against the wall preparing to fight. If that door opened, he would knock them flying and run.

Storm crouched in the vegetation. The disgraced teenagers banished from the beach were being escorted back to Tyne Island by the patrol. Leaving the rucksack in the hidden boat Storm crept through the greenery. Ahead was a building half submerged into the hillside like a hobbit house. A sign in bold letters said: 'WATER TREATMENT PLANT' 'KEEP OUT!' She imagined that it was rarely visited. The last location recorded for Finn had been on Fenton Isle, fairly near the beach. This was an ideal place to hide him. Looking around her surroundings for any activity she saw only dense forest. The place was deserted.

Bending low, Storm ran to the fence line that surrounded the plant. Taking out wire cutters from her tool belt, she cut a big enough line in the green wire fence for her and Finn to pass through. The spare wire in one of the pouches must be used after, to disguise the means of entry. Storm squeezed through the wire and ran swiftly to a shabby wooden door with another: 'NO ENTRY!" sign on it. In case people hadn't got the message from the initial sign on the fence.

Pressing her ear to the wood, Storm heard a mild humming like machinery and a shrill scratching noise near the hinges of the door. Excitement coursed through Storm. It must be Finn trying to dig his way out. Either that or a tall mouse. Taking the penknife from the tool belt she pulled out a Phillips screwdriver attachment. Inserting it into the indent of the screws that held the hinges on, she pressed in hard, rotating it. The screws began to loosen. The perilous situation they were in called for Storm to keep as quiet as possible. As the screws loosened, the scratching stopped. Storm glanced around her periodically, checking for security or other signs of life. Fortunately, there were none. Finally, the screws were all undone and Storm pushed against the door with all her weight.

There was a bang and the door opened off its hinges. Finn stood, ready to attack. A small slim figure stood in the doorway. It was Storm.

"Oh my God." Finn hugged her. "You came! I knew you would!"

"Oh, Finn your face!" Storm was horrified to see the swollen cheek, and black eye. "I should have let you know it was me outside. Must have scared you!"

Finn smiled and winced with pain.

"No, you did the right thing. Better to be super quiet and not call out. We need to go. They'll be back." Finn whispered. "They're desperate to find you."

"I know." Storm nodded. "Tell you later, how I know. Let's keep quiet."

Hastily replacing and tightening the screws, the door looked as it had upon arrival. Finn ruffled any flattened grass as they crept back to the fence, Finn just managing to fit though the gap. Taking the spare wire Storm deftly wove it around the area she had cut, pressing it together.

"Good as new." Finn whispered.

Covering their tracks might earn them precious minutes. They needed to escape!   Hastily they headed back through the vegetation to the hidden boat. Sitting on the grass, Storm gave Finn some water. He gulped it greedily.

"Got any food. Bloody starving! Was torture!"

Storm grinned handing him some cheese and onion pasties.

"They didn't feed you."

Finn shook his head. Wolfing the food, he swallowed more water.

"Had a wee bit of a mars bar but that's all-in days! Bodies gone into shock! That's so much better." He finished the last pasty frowning. "The boats so risky though Storm. I just can't see us making it undetected."

"I agree. I brought the diving gear."

Finn's blue eyes gleamed, widening with surprise.

"We could wear the diving gear and swim, taking the boat with us. Like holding on to it to preserve air and pushing it. It'll hide us. If detected, they'll think it's just a boat adrift, that one of the students forgot to tie up properly. We can duck dive and swim together to Tyne Island. Then decide what to do from there."

Storm nodded.

"We're on the same page." Storm said excitedly. Her teeth chattered in terror, at the thought of it.

"Have you charge in your phone?" Finn asked.

"Nah. It's dead. Fell out of a tree and smashed."

Finn's eyebrows shot up.

"Long story. We've both so much to tell. Need to get out of here."

"Dude with the balaclava smashed mine to pieces. Don't know anyone's numbers. Do you?"

"Nah. Totally no clue." Storm shook her head.

"Gangs gonna be checking out railway, bus, everything." Finn frowned.

"We'll get away from this place, then we can make a plan Finn. "It's pretty rural we can stick to countryside 'til we get further away enough to get a train back home."

"One step at a time."

Storm nodded. Unpacking the wet suits and diving kit, they placed their clothes in the heavy plastic and sealed it with tape Storm had brought.

"Really impressed." Finn nodded at the plastic and tool belt. "I'll take the rucksack."

They waited until nightfall then clipping the cylinders onto belts they headed off, moving the boat down the beach into the water. Storm ran back removing any trace of them. If someone looked thoroughly, they would see the broken branches but at a glance it looked undisturbed.

Paddling out to sea they pushed the rowing boat in front of them, using the lights from the cabins and huts on Tyne Island as a guide. Nearing Tyne Island they heard a shout.

"Identify yourself! You in the boat NOW!"

Finn clipped the end of a bungy cord onto Storm's belt and the other end onto his and whispered:

"Slowly on three. One, two, three."

They carefully dived down into the blackness. Storm kept up with Finn and followed his lead. The water felt freezing on her feet, hands and face. Travelling blind, primitive instincts led the way. The water became shallow and they broke the surface. Turning off air, Finn took out his mouth piece.

They were situated at the far side of the island. Lights and voices shouted in the distance around the abandoned boat.

"Got enough air Storm. Barely used any thanks to the boat. Mainland's not far, about a mile."

"Let's do it but head away from the quay. Too obvious and busy. If they get us we've had it anyway. I'd rather drown with you Finn. Remember seeing some nature place on 'maps' over to the left. Our best bet. Head there yeah. There's some small islands on the way just like tiny grasslands."

"Let's go. Same drill as before."

Replacing the mouthpieces, they changed direction and submerging once more, headed towards the left side of the mainland. This time Finn activated the underwater torch. It was surreal travelling through strange waters. The estuary was mud based and the water was murky with strange plants and moss growing amidst the mud banks and rocks. They stopped a couple of times for a rest before reaching the grass mounds of tiny nature islands scattered across the bay. Preserving air and breath, they didn't speak, resubmerging until finally they came to shallows, arriving on a gritty beach. A sign read: 'Arne Nature Reserve'.

Finn pointed ahead and they crept up the beach, passing through a small woodland littered with stones and fallen sticks that led into a meadow with a stream threaded through it. There they stopped and peeled off the wetsuits, changing into their dry clothes.

"Can't believe we made it." said Finn. "Almost out of air too. "

"So far so good." Storm nodded. "Feet are sore, from the woods."

"Same!" nodded Finn.

They washed their feet in the stream before putting on thick socks and boots. Munching sausage rolls from Storms endless food supply, they strode across the fields. They had to get as far away as possible from Fenton Isle even if it meant walking all night.

"What I'd give for a hot chocolate!" said Finn.

"I know. Sitting up in that tree all I could think of was you and I sitting in the Emerald Pool Chamber drinking hot chocolate. I was so scared!"

"We'll get back there soon Storm, to Puffin Island." Finn said reassuringly.

"I hope so." Storm said wistfully.

"You think they know I'm gone yet?" Finn asked anxiously.

"Dunno. From their point of view. They don't know where I am, and think you're locked in that room with no means of escape. Plus, a tall fence that's also padlocked and security patrols. Hopefully they'll just leave you there 'til morning. They obviously think the Fenton Isle is a secure prison or they would have posted a guard."

"Hope so. It's when they discover I'm gone......." he said quietly running his fingers through his hair.

"I know. Think they've got drones?" Storm was also worried. "Ones with heat sensors?"

"Bloody hope not. If we stay clear of any CCTV, leave no tracks and hide somewhere remote, but where there are other people about, we'll be ok. We need to get hold of a phone."

Storm fished hers out of her pocket. It was still black and inactive. Sharing stories of the gruesome events of the past few days they talked as they walked, making good progress.

"There's this old, abandoned village near one of the army camps. If we head, there. I kinda remember where it is from 'maps'. The army used it during the war for training. Evicted all the residents. Some of it's bombed out, but I think there's an old church intact." Storm said.

"Like that's not sinister as." Finn smiled and winced.

"That looks so painful Finn."

Finns' cheek was purple.

"Totally is. Lucky it's just bruised." He sneezed. "Aw the pain."

"We'll head there. To the old sinister abandoned church."

"Sounds like a plan. Think I'm gonna move into the Locked Room when we get back. Just to feel safe for a bit."

"I hear you, totally. I will too." Storm agreed. "I feel bad."

"Why?"

"I feel totally pissed at Dad."

Finn looked relieved.

"Don't feel bad. Same. Totally pissed off with my old man. Second time he's put me, us, in danger. Least last time he was in the Locked Room keeping an eye. This time.... Storm they were going to kill us for what happened on Puffin Island. Even if they got the money back. For revenge and to punish our dads."

Storm nodded.

"I know." She said quietly.

Finn took her hand. Wearily they stumbled on, too tired even to chatter. They couldn't risk being captured again. The men had means, but Storm and Finn were determined. Their mission was now to return to Puffin Island, and no one would be allowed to get in their way.

CHAPTER 15

The House

Dawn broke. The dark sky was streaked with cobalt blue, white and streaks of red. Finn yawned loudly.

"Wow, you have a big mouth." Storm commented. "My feet are dying!"

Finn grinned. His stomach rumbled a deep growl.

"Same. My insides are like touching each other. Got any more food?" Finn asked hopefully.

"No, for the hundredth time! Need to find a shop."

"And get caught on CCTV or by someone spying."

"What's that there?" Storm pointed to a white building in the distance. "Shop maybe, or a pub?"

"Looks like a shop. Can see the red and white sign, Corf Store."

"You can see that!"

Finn nodded.

Nearing the road, they crept cautiously forward, before racing across the road, one by one. A 'Closed' sign hung on the inside of the door. The opening times: 0800 – 1900. The shop was small and resembled a cabin, with white wooden cladding. Leaflets from local businesses and clubs were stuck to the windows.

"Not open for an hour. Let's have a scout." Finn squinted through the window. A clock hung on the wall. "Oh, I can see food! Cornish pasties, beef slices. Oh my God!" He exclaimed.

"What?" Storm asked in alarm.

"Chocolate cake and milk in the fridge."

"You're like a dog salivating over a bone." Storm laughed. Her stomach too was empty and making strange whining noises.

"Salivating. Get you Storm.!" Finn looked impressed.

The sound of an engine in the distance prompted them to hide out of view.

"We're like totally distracted. Hungry, and food obsessed! They'll know we'll need something to eat. Especially since you had nothing but an old Mars bar from them. How many shops around here?" whispered Storm.

"Don't remind me. Not sure can ever eat one again! Loads of shops in Poole town." replied Finn.

"That'll buy us a few hours if we're lucky. If they don't find us there, they'll widen the search."

Running to the back of the shop they discovered a shabby white door with paint peeling and a sign pinned to it that read: 'Deliveries!'. A small window led to the stock room. It was shut.

"Reckon you can fit?" Finn asked. "If we can get supplies or even a phone we can disappear and might even be able to get some help."

"Even if I grind my bones to dust, I'll get in." said Storm determinedly.

Taking off her boots, thick hoody and tool belt she looked tiny.

"You've dumped a heap load of weight Storm. What the actual..."

"You're surprised! It's stress and walking nine hundred miles!"

"Yeah, stress'll do it, that and being kidnapped and nearly murdered." Finn reached up and ran the blade of the pen knife manipulating the catch of the old metal framed window. It pinged open. He pulled out the waistband of his joggers. "I'm wasting away too!"

Lifting the window Storm squeezed through.

"Ouch my shins!" Storm winced as old iron grated her shins. She landed with a crash on the white chest freezer below the window.

"Elegant." smirked Finn.

Storm pulled a face. Opening the storage fridge, she took out a four pint bottle of milk, chicken and mushroom pasties, chocolate cake, sausages, butter, bread, hot chocolate powder and chocolate bars. Giving Finn a thumbs up, she called to him:

"There's a small folded up rucksack in the big one."

Finn rummaged and held it open at the gap in the window.

"Hurry Storm!"

The traffic was getting heavier, progressing from the odd passing vehicle to a steady stream of cars, lorries, and motor bikes. Finn frowned. It was Monday morning. Only three days since they'd left Puffin Island. Seemed like an eternity!

Storm was stuffing everything useful that she could find, into the bag. Carefully she handed it through the window. Taking a fifty-pound note from the stash, she placed it under a tin of beans to pay for the groceries.

"Just wiping the scene." she called.

Using a tea towel from the supply for sale, she wiped down where her fingers had touched and clambered back out of the window, wincing as the metal dug once more into her stomach and legs. Finn closed the window while Storm redressed.

Hastily they moved further from the road to the woods at the back of the shop. Storm carried the food on her back and Finn had the large black rucksack. Clambering over a three-bar wooden fence they disappeared into more woods and meadows.

"That wood." Finn pointed to a dense forest ahead. "About half a mile cross that field. We'll stop there and eat."

"Yeah, go in deep. Might be our last chance before they come searching for us." Storm said. "They're not gonna go to all that bother and just give up!"

"No, sadly."

Deep in the thick of the bronze woods, Finn propped some fallen branches against a tree for added cover. The tree trunk was massive, hundreds of years old. The branches were entangled with the other trees in the forest and the sky shone a glinting emerald, yellow and red. Sitting on a bin bag Storm unloaded a tiny camp stove fuelled by a fire lighter. Clearing leaves from the woodland floor, she placed the stove on it.

"It's a risk but we need hot food and drink." Storm declared decisively.

She was worried about Finn, for despite his bravado he looked gaunt, thin, and tired. Pouring milk into the metal mess tin, she added hot chocolate bringing it to the boil before pouring thick chocolate liquid into the two flask cups that she'd added to the kit at the last minute. Sipping the sweet richness, Finn moaned in ecstasy as the heat flowed down his body pooling comfort into an empty raw belly. Washing out the tin with water, Storm added butter and sausages. Sizzling, the waft of food wrapped around their senses.

"Oh, the smell!" Finn was in heaven.

"Let's hope we're the only ones who smell it." Storm glanced nervously around her. Breaking a roll, she dipped the two halves into the butter and stuffing it full of thin sausages handed it to Finn before making one for herself. Silence reigned. Only the sound of the birds chattering and chirping and the odd buzz of a fly while they ate.

Storm cleared away the stove, mess tin and repacked the rucksacks. Placing the leaves over where the stove had been there was no obvious evidence of them having been there.

"We need to move Finn." said Storm morosely. Her legs ached with fatigue.

"I just need to sleep." he said. "So, so tired." He closed his eyes.

"We're not far enough yet Finn." insisted Storm. "If they catch us you'll get plenty of sleep."

"How so?"

"How so? Plenty of sleep when you're dead!"

"Oh nice! How edgy of you." mumbled Finn. "God damn." Grumpily he clambered to his feet. The ordeal was beginning to take its toll.

"Bit more distance, then we'll find somewhere to camp."

Ruins appeared in the distance. It looked like an old castle.

"That the place we're heading?" Finn stumbled.

"Nah, it's further. Might need to stop someplace else though. I'm really struggling too. That village is further than I thought. No way we're gonna make it in one hit."

Hiking further they crossed a yellow meadow. At a small lane, a sign for 'The Blue Pool - 2 miles' was followed by an arrow. Tourist information on a small glass enclosed plague told them that the pool was magical, full of a medicinal cocktail of minerals accompanied by a picture of a deep blue pool surrounded by forest.

"Nice. Bit like our Emerald Pool Chamber." commented Storm. "I wonder if we've got time for a visit."

"Time out, on the run, to visit the beautiful sights of Dorset." Finn snapped. "Really!"

"Truth!" Storm nodded. "No need to be a dick about it."

"Sorry. Exhausted and cranky as."

The sound of helicopter rotators sounded in the distance. Storm and Finn ran through wild grasses scattering butterflies, to the safety of surrounding forest. Ahead was a field with horses. Four bay thoroughbreds were grazing. A barn doubled as an upper storage area for hay and a lower shelter for the horses from the elements, when they were out to grass.

Hurrying they scrambled over the five-bar gate into the field. The horses pricked up their ears and looked over, whickering, before returning to munch lush grass. Heading to the barn Storm climbed hastily up the ladder taking the heavy rucksack from Finn. At the back of the shelter, they rearranged a few hay bales to hide them from prying eyes. Through a crack in the roof, Storm could see a helicopter circulating a wide radius. This was a good time to sleep. They couldn't be seen from the air. Drones were expensive and would be a last resort. They had a few hours to sleep before their journey continued.

Storm awoke with a start. Rain squeezed through the thin gap in the planks dripping onto her face. Disorientated, for a moment she thought the soft hay was her bed and that she was asleep in her cosy round bedroom. Sitting up on her elbow she shook Finn.

"Finn."

A whining nose sounded overhead, then disappeared.

Finn mumbled in his sleep. Storm put her hand over his mouth to silence him. Opening his eyes he looked up at her. She put her finger to her lip pointing upwards. The sound gradually disappeared.

"Drone?" said Finn sitting up.

"Maybe?" Storm crawled to where the horses were gathered below in the shelter. "The horses will have disguised us from any infra-red heat sensors."

"Do you think they even have drones, eye in the sky, and all that?"

Storm nodded.

"Defo better to think so. That white yacht in the Firth of Forth was like massive. They're loaded. They can defo afford a drone. Wouldn't be surprised if they're ex-military gone rogue. Looked it."

"Great!" said Finn. "Two teenagers against the dark world of organised crime. Military trained. Think Air Cadets counts? No clue what the time is."

Storm yawned.

"Counts for something. We've got this far. Have to head off Finn. They'll search different areas so won't be back here for a while. Have no clue what time it is. Kinda weird not knowing."

"Taxi! Wonder how much one is to Scotland!"

Storm laughed.

"That's actually not the worst idea... taxi then train some of the way. Just staying off the radar's the thing."

"Yeah, we'll take another route back. Carlise or somewhere on the way?"

"Yeah, they'll totally be checking trains to Edinburgh. I reckon. Have to play it by ear."

Leaving the sanctuary of the shelter, they climbed over another fence and crossed grassland before disappearing once more into the forest.

"What I'd give for a hot chocolate. Starving!" moaned Finn. "Sick of traipsing."

"Same."

"Shh what's that?" whispered Finn.

"What?" Hissed Storm frantically. "What's what?"

"That weird noise."

They paused like startled deer.

"Oh my God it's traffic! There must be a road up ahead." cried Finn.

A fence of three wires, formed a barrier between the woodland and the grey concrete road surface.

"It looks like a major road." Finn crept forward. "Masses of traffic. We need to be super careful. If they suspect we're heading cross country, they'll be scouting the area in case we're hitching a lift."

"Is that a petrol station up there?" Storm pointed to a yellow and red sign in the distance to the right.

"Yeah. We need to get across this road. Have to wait 'til there's zero traffic Storm."

"I know. It's risky."

Lush woodland lay opposite. The road ran through a part of the nature reserve.

A black sports car zoomed past. Then the gift of silence.

"Now!" Storm ordered.

Scrambling through the wire fence they pelted across the road diving into bracken on the other side.

"Garage could sell phones." said Finn excitedly.

"Yeah, got our sim cards. Could phone home, hide out and just sit waiting to be rescued. Imagine being picked up in Pop's Aston Martin. Be back on Puffin Island in no time. "

"Warm an' cosy up in the Zen room huddled in front of the log burner…"

"Looking out across the ocean, drinking hot chocolate, scoffing chicken sandwiches. Masses of hot chips with salt and tomato sauce."

Finn's stomach let out a loud and very long growl.

"Oh my God! This is actual torture. We need to find out where we are, get a phone, and a map just in case." He looked anxiously up at the sky. "It's getting awful dark. Storm's brewing Storm."

Storm grinned.

"You used to always say that."

"When life wasn't so mental."

"Let's head closer." Storm nodded over to the garage in the distance.

They crept through the undergrowth. A steady drizzle fell. Storm tightened the drawstring of her hoody, shivering. Their legs were soaking wet. Crouching around the back of the building, they surveyed traffic pulling up at the petrol station. Motorists were busy filling tanks, washing cars or shopping in the small store for groceries.

A black four-wheel drive with tinted windows pulled up at one of the pumps. A bald man climbed out and began filling the car.

Storm visibly jumped clutching hold of Finn's arm. He looked at her in alarm.

"That dude…. the buff one with no hair…he's one of the guys I saw when I was up the tree, for sure!"

The bald man called out to someone in the car, as he strode to the garage shop, on his way to pay for the fuel.

"You wanting fags yeah?"

"Yeah, forty." A gruff Welsh accent replied.

"Balaclava!" Finn exclaimed. "I recognise that voice anywhere!"

"The dude who punched you?"

Finn nodded. His swollen face boasted a tinge of yellow around the purple bruise.

"Stay down." He put a hand restraining Storm on her arm.

The bald man re-emerged, and the vehicle pulled away at speed heading off to the left.

"What better time." Storm sprinted to the garage before Finn could talk her out of it.

The rainfall was heavy, and she stood with the other miserable shoppers in the queue dripping puddles onto the floor, hoods up, heads down. Paying for the goods, she walked briskly back to Finn. Hastily, they disappeared back into the forest.

"You absolute lunatic!" Finn vented, tripping over a fallen log.

Storm grinned.

"Couldn't have been a safer time! After they just left!" She said confidently.

"Unless they planted a bug of sorts." Finn snapped, rubbing his shin.

"Paranoia getting out of hand." Storm commented. "Can't plant bugs at every random petrol station Finn!"

"You scared the actual shit out of me Storm! Longest ten minutes of my life!"

"Worse news!"

"What now?" Finn frowned.

"It's five o'clock."

"What do you mean five o'clock?"

"The time. Finn! It's five pm! We slept most of the day! It's gonna be dark soon. Lost a whole day!"

"What the actual...No wonder it's dark and gloomy looking." He looked up at the stone-grey sky.

"And to be totally grim! More bad news. The shop guy had the telly on and the weather forcast's tragic. A bad storm and weather warnings!"

"Oh, it gets better!" Finn muttered shaking his head with disbelief.

"Exactly. Thunder and lightning!"

"Very very frightening!" Finn finished off. "Seriously this is bad. What's in the bag?"

"Map of the area. We've made good progress. We're near the

village and there's some small railway station just beyond it." She suddenly smiled holding up a box. "Cheap phone! Need to charge it asap."

"Yes!" Finn hugged her. "Yes! Yes! Yes! You actual star! Tell me you brought the battery charger."

"I did."

Stopping, they crouched down in the vegetation. The pitter pattering of water cascading from the dark clouds onto the leaves. Storm rummaged frantically through the black rucksack, rustling the thick plastic as she searched for the battery phone charger.

"Oh no!" Her hand went to her mouth. "Noooo!"

"What!"

"You absolute utter utter moron!" She cried in anguish.

"Thanks!" Finn was confused.

"No, me! Me! I am!" She wailed.

Unzipping the side pocket of the damp rucksack, she pulled out the battery charger. Water dripped from it. Storm sat down heavily onto the orange, yellow and green carpet of autumnal leaves and began to cry in frustration and despair.

"I completely forgot I hadn't packed it in the main bit. Finn I've screwed up majorly. It's ruined."

"Hey. It might dry out." He said shaking the water from it.

"It's been submerged in salt water! In the actual sea. Salt's like corrosive." Storm clutched her head in distress. "Like my phone didn't ever work again after it got wet."

"You dropped it out of a tree." said Finn reasonably.

"I'm a disaster. Can't do anything. Destroyed two phones and our only chance. So done with this. Hate my life." Storm screamed hurling the offensive charger at a tree.

Finn picked up the pieces and put them back in the pouch. He went to hug her, but the manic glare from her eyes changed his mind.

"We need to get going. Storm! Be ok. It will. We're together." he said gently. "I'd be dead now if it wasn't for you rescuing me, remember that. And you did that, whilst battling with your anxiety which is major. Pretty good job in my book."

Storm looked at him and sniffed wiping her nose and tears on the black hoody.

"Just all too much." She looked up at the sky and breathed out a long breath.

"I know. Feel the same, too be honest." Finn shook his head. "Been a real rough time, Storm. Ends in sight. Let's keep it together."

Storm climbed reluctantly to her feet. In silence they walked on, into the increasing dimness, as the light of the day diminished.

A deep rumbling grumbled in the distance. Storm stopped for a drink of water. Plink, plonk, plink, plink, plink resonated as rain drops fell hitting the plastic of the bottle. Dusk dawned, darkening the undergrowth. A half-moon peeked through wispy grey clouds that floated intermittently dimming natures torch of luna brilliance.

Mysterious twilight brought with it the gateway to a new sinister world of shadows. As the last light crept away, they passed through the veil from light into darkness. Scuttling, and screams filled the air. Storm jumped, bracing.

"What the hell was that?" She flicked on the small torch.

Black transformed to greens, beige and dancing shadows.

"Just a fox. Better keep that off as much as possible." Finn whispered sneezing five times in a row.

"Bless you." Storm turned off the light. "My nerves are totally dying."

They tried to use torchlight as little as possible. Storm

estimated, by the landmarks they noted along the way that they were nearly at the abandoned village. Once there, they would rest and try to get to the train station undetected. Once on the train they could charge up the phone. Frustration aside, there was hope.

The woodland became dense with hundreds of trees standing in rows with their branches twisted and knotted. The interior was pitch black and the torch beam, was activated to guide the way. The mossy mud floor was a mass of twigs covered by an autumnal rug of gold, green, rust and burgundy. The wooded hill became steeper with each footstep taken.

Finn stopped.

"What is it?" Storm asked, scared.

"Really not feeling too good." Finn said. "Head feels fuzzy. Just want to sleep."

Storm nodded invisibly in the dimness. Feeling Finn's forehead. He was burning up, hot and clammy at the same time.

"Need to get to a safe place. Tomorrow, maybe we should call the police."

"Can't Storm." Said Finn. "Be ok just feeling a bit shit."

"We're still in Dorset Finn!" Storm uttered with frustration. "Take us about five hundred years to get back to Puffin Island!"

"Yeah but, nearly out of the woods!"

"Oh funny." Storm laughed. "We need heat, food, sleep then we'll be ok."

"Tomato soup. Aw remember in the Emerald Pool Chamber, with cheese sandwiches dipped in! I can almost smell pork chops! Jacket potatoes stuffed with cheese and ham." Finn obsessed.

BANG! Thunder cracked overhead and the whole woodland lit up with a vast illumination of sheet lightening. Startled. They glanced at each other for reassurance.

"Nearly at the top." Shouted Finn pointing to a wooden fence about four meters away. "No worries love being stuck in a wood with lightning!"

"Least it's not fork!"

Scrambling up the steep hill they reached the top as another flash of lightening lit up the area, followed by a violent cracking, as thunder rolled. The fence post displayed a sign that read. TYNE ESTATE. A 'FOR SALE' sign stood by it. Lightening flashed again. An old mansion stood in radiance. Rain began to fall steadily. Storm and Finn stood staring at the house swathed in darkness.

The building was golden and rectangular. The brickwork rounded on each side leading upwards to two vast turrets. Battlements joined them. Large arched windows sat in the towers, with seven smaller ones beneath on the first floor of the building. Storm and Finn walked towards the mansion.

"Great! A haunted house to add to the mix." Said Finn.

"Take my chances with a bunch of ghosts any day." replied Storm. "Rather that than those psychos."

"Same."

On the ground floor the windows were tall and square with two on each side of the front door that was a gothic arch with stain glass at the top. The door was made of a thick oak. Shining torchlight into the window they saw that there was sparse furniture.

"This must be the lounge." Finn shone the light on an inglenook fireplace and old battered chesterfield sofa, discarded and left.

The floor was parquet, hundreds of pieces of gleaming rectangular wooden slabs fitted together. There were faded patches on the walls where paintings had once proudly hung.

"Empty for sure." He nodded.

Moving around to the back of the building, a smaller older

window sat in what appeared to be a larder. Finn, using the blade of the penknife once more, managed to prise it open. Picking up Storm, he lifted her up to the high window, where she placed one leg and shoulder in first before bending her neck and head through, the small space. Shining the beam around, the larder was empty and shelved. Storm used the shelves as a ladder to climb down.

Entering the inwards of the sinister spooky mansion, Storm had expected to be terrified, but the house gave off a surprisingly warm ambience. The kitchen was vast and marble with a breakfast bar island in the middle. She wondered what secrets the old house held. The walls would have many tales to tell. Flicking the light switch nothing happened. The electricity had been disconnected.

The kitchen door was locked but an old key sat in the lock of the back door that led out to the outbuildings. Storm let Finn in. Together they moved through the old house. Flashes of lightening showed gleaming floors, a vast white marble staircase with black iron rails leading upwards.

"Electric's off." Storm whispered. "Don't reckon it's haunted. Feels nice."

"Edgy. Have a look around and then food." Finn pulled out the big torch from the rucksack. "Least if electrics off it kinda proves no-ones living here."

"Finn there's no furniture!"

"Yeah but...you know what I mean." He gave her a sidelong glance. "And ghosts are the least of our worries. I'll snuggle up with the Tyne Estate ghost anytime rather than face Balaclava the Bully again."

Leaving the bags in the hall, they wandered through a huge library devoid of books, just row upon row of shelves encased in glass. Fireplaces with cream mantlepieces dominated each room.

"Study maybe." Storm opened a door poking her head inside.

"Ballroom?" said Finn, opening the door of another.

A vast room with waxed floors and wooden wall panels was a place to fill with fun and laughter. The interior wall opposite the French doors was mirrored reflecting light from the picture windows and glittering crystal chandeliers.

The first floor had ten bedrooms with fireplaces and en-suite bathrooms of shiny grey, cream and white with mirrors, and gleaming towel rails.

"It's like modern as." Said Finn. "If we sold some treasure, we could buy this. Share it."

"Which turret do you want for your room, left or right?"

"Right!"

Heading up to the Turret rooms, Storm swung the beam around the carpeted area.

"Surprisingly big. Reminds me of my bedroom." She signed wistfully. "Don't think I could stand a square bedroom again after the Lighthouse Tower."

The sudden roar of a helicopter sounded. Appearing out of the storm it circled the building. Storm and Finn threw themselves to the floor. The thunder had disguised the sound of its approach. Finn lay on the torch as he fumbled to turn it off. Lights shone in the windows before disappearing into the chaos of the night.

"Owner or Balaclava?"

"Place is empty. Unless they have someone to check it. I think gang."

Rain lashed against the windows.

"Jez they must be desperate. Unless..."

"Our Dad's?"

"Possible they're looking for us; but we don't know, so it's too big a risk. The gang will kill us, it's worth remembering. And with military backgrounds we can't distinguish if the Heli is the good guys or the bad!"

"Totally worth remembering!" said Finn pointing to his cheek. "Mild punishment, think Balaclava said."

"How you feeling?"

"Shit. Frozen, wet, starving, need to sleep."

"Heli's gone. Let's head down to the room with the sofa."

The neglected living room had white wooden shutters at each window. Storm ordered Finn to lie on the sofa. She closed the shutters. Heading to the outbuildings near the kitchen, she'd spied a log store during their earlier reconnaissance. Filling an old basket with twigs and logs she brought it in and built a fire in the grate. Flames flickered, licking the wood, hissing, and crackling. Warmth and cheer filled the cream walls. The house was happy to have occupants once more. Peeling off their wet clothes they laid them near the heat where they dried out, steaming.

Storm lit the emergency candles and set up the small stove on the flagstone surrounding the fireplace.

"And we have…drum roll!" Storm pulled a tin dramatically out of the bag holding it up in the air. "Tomato soup!"

"You absolute hero!" Finn sneezed violently.

The thunder had decreased in volume and velocity heading out to sea. Rain fell steadily.

They sat staring into the purple, yellow flames, drinking soup and eating pasties. After a pudding of chocolate cake with milk, Finn's eyes closed, and he slept deeply. Storm covered him with her dried coat, as he had bare legs and no change of trousers. Adding more wood to the fire Storm curled into a ball on the floor using the rucksack as a lumpy pillow.

Visualising Puffin Island, she mused that mere months ago her terror had been Shelley High School and staying away from home. It was strange that she could cope with fleeing from gangsters and being on the run, a truly fearful situation, but the prospect of the routine and pressure of attending school was too much for her to bear. People were complex with different strengths and weaknesses, and things they excelled at. At least she'd made progress, learning to control her anxiety. She'd travelled down to Dorset on her own, rescued Finn, and was now spending yet another night away from home! Tomorrow the mission was to get to a train station without fail. They were nearly out of food. Whatever challenges Tuesday brought, they would face them head on. Storm's eyelids slowly closed, and she drifted off to sleep.

CHAPTER 16
The Battle of Waterloo

Storm awoke to the sound of a diesel engine running outside. Leaping to her feet, she peeked through the white shutters. The black 4x4 spotted at the petrol station, was parked outside! There were four men leaning against it, smoking, and chatting. They were stocky, and bald headed.

"Finn!" hissed Storm. "Quick, get dressed!" She threw his dry clothes at him.

Finn awoke with a start. Dressing rapidly, they gathered their belongings, stuffing them into the black rucksack.

Storm raised her hands in despair, gesturing to the embers in the grate.

"Back door. There are outbuildings, and woods. Head out there."

"They'll know someone's been here. Nothing we can do." said Finn, glancing out at the vehicle parked on the gravelled drive.

Storm grabbed the heavy rucksack, passing it to Finn as they tiptoed to the back of the mansion. Quietly opening the back door, Finn removed the key and locked the door behind them. Any delays for the gang were important. Moving to the back of the outbuildings, they had a view of the men, who were in deep discussion, gesticulating to the house and fields. The abandoned village lay to their left. Storm pointed in that direction.

Finn held up his hand for her to wait. The men were striding around the property looking for an access point. They stopped at the larder window examining it, shaking their heads. Balaclava discovered the weakest part of the house, the old back door. Standing back, he kicked it in. With a loud bang it swung on its hinges. The men disappeared into the mansion.

"Wait!" whispered Finn.

Picking up discarded wood with jagged nails sticking through, that lay by the woodstore, Finn crouched down, racing to where the shiny black vehicle was parked. It would have to be reversed to return to the road, so he placed the wood behind the back tyres, sharp rusty nails pointing upwards, just touching the rubber. A puncture in two tyres would cause a much-needed interruption. Slashing the wheels with his penknife would be too obvious a sabotage.

Running back to Storm, they paused for a moment before crawling on their stomachs into the undergrowth.

"Need to get to a railway station now." Finn whispered frantically. "It's getting too dangerous! We've got to get out of here. Being on foot is a major disadvantage."

"I know. Everything we've done, and they've still caught up with us!"

Taking precious moments, they checked the map.

"Grange Road, then Corfe Road, erm, Wareham Station.... around six miles. Need to head straight on." Storm pointed ahead.

Passing derelict cottages on the left, they jogged lethargically through the woodland. The day was bright and sunny, and they followed a dog walkers' path through the maze of brownish grey trees. The woodland was ablaze with orange, gold, and green leaves. It was like ambling through a rustic painting. A thatched cottage loomed up on the right in the distance, situated across a narrow lane. It boasted a neat garden full of late roses of red, peach and cream. A white picket fence surrounded the property. Leaning up against the fence were three bicycles. Two adult sized and one child's pink bike.

"What direction do we need to go?" Finn asked.

"To our right."

"We need transport. Leave some money for the bikes." He called softly.

Finn moved the child's bike forward while Storm put two hundred pounds under a rock in the small basket. Taking the adult bikes, they wheeled them out of sight of the cottage, before mounting them.

"Top speed Storm. This is major risk!"

They whizzed along the country lanes, down slopes, and up hills, peddling furiously. Intermittent signposts for Wareham spurred them on. Storm's thighs were burning with exertion as she desperately tried to keep up with Finn. Two miles to go. No sign of Balaclava and his gang. Then one mile and a sign for the train station. Finally, they arrived at Wareham Station.

"Legs like jelly." Storm panted, propping the bike up against the metal railings of the bike shed.

"Same." Finn left his bike, and they made their way into the small station. "Feel all weird and wobbly."

"Waterloo, arrival two minutes." Storm exclaimed excitedly staring up at the TV screen that displayed arrivals and departures. "Takes two hours twenty-nine minutes."

They bought tickets and made their way out onto the grey platform.

An automated voice announced the arrival of the London Waterloo train. Screeching and groaning, the train snaked into the station. With relief Storm and Finn boarded, sitting in window seats away from the platform edge.

"Can't believe we made it."

Finn nodded. He looked dazed. Shaking his head. Storm handed him the remainder of the bottle of water. He drank thirstily.

"Aw that's better. Majorly traumatic! Won't rest 'til we're back on Puffin Island, Storm."

"Same."

Finn pointed to the power point on the side of the train wall under the table.

"Oh my God! Electric. We can charge the phone. Where's the food bag? You did bring it!"

Storm turned visibly pale!

"I must have left it by the old sofa." Storm shook her head. "Totally freaked by Balaclava and the rest of them turning up. Panicking about the fire and leaving traces...and getting out of there...know it's no excuse!" She looked out of the window, biting her lip.

"Storm, I'd have left the big bag too in total panic." Finn kicked the rucksack. "It was actually terrifying seeing them all standing outside the house, smoking, planning."

"They'll know we were there."

"Would have been clued up anyway Storm, footprints, fire, all sorts gave it away." Finn ran his fingers through his dark hair. "Can't always cover our tracks. We've done what we could. They're serious criminals. Gangsters! Evil!"

"I suppose."

"What else was in there?"

"You'll hate me."

"Come on?"

"About two pints of milk, half a chocolate cake, packet of sausages, rolls, butter and the phone. Plus, a heap of chocolate. Nothing else...It's all in the big bag."

"Hmmm that's a seriously, nearly hateable offence losing all that food, especially the chocolate cake!" Finn grinned. "But as you saved me from a long slow torturous death, I'll forgive you."

"Thanks!" Storm laughed. "Seriously though. It's all getting a bit too intense!"

Finn nodded.

"It is. All a bit too much." He sneezed into his sleeve.

"How are you feeling?" Storm asked.

"Better. Think it was that stuff they used to put me to sleep. Made my throat and nose feel all weird."

"Must have been so scary Finn." Storm said sympathetically. "It's maybe your system clearing all the crap out."

"Yeah. I knew there was something off about that Adrian and Tom his stepdad. Just had this heavy uncomfortable feeling." He patted his gut. "Shouldn't have followed him out to the bay 'cause I knew…knew something bad was gonna happen. It's hard when it's someone senior like a teacher, to say 'No'!"

"I know that feeling." Storm agreed.

They fell quiet watching the landscape speed before their eyes.

The train slowed and an announcement declared that they would shortly be arriving at London Waterloo. Ten minutes later they pulled into the station.

"Look out for the bald dudes." warned Finn.

Storm nodded.

London Waterloo Station was packed with hardened commuters, wired from a busy day at the office. Charging into the entrance business people, anxiously checked the arrival and departure boards for cancellations or delays that would affect their routine and journey home. Smartly dressed, with glazed eyes, their minds were still connected to laptops, now stuffed into black material handheld cases.

Storm and Finn walked swiftly from the arrival platform through the internal ticket barriers. Weaving through crowds, buzzing around the shopping area, they headed towards the taxi rank.

"Will follow our plan. Cost us but be worth it." Said Storm dodging a woman with a buggy containing a screaming baby.

Commuters were tut tutting glaring at the infant, as if it were an alien dropped from the sky.

"Too right it'll cost ya!" A gruff southern English accent sounded in Finn's ear. A vice like grip held his arm.

The smell of stale coffee and cigarettes emanated from hot breath panting onto his ear lobe.

"Storm run!" Shouted Finn loudly.

Startled commuters spun around trying to locate the source of the commotion. Storm also looked around screaming with fright as she spotted Balaclava standing close to Finn, for she could see what others couldn't, a black Glock pistol pointing at her cousins back.

Welsh, Balaclava's gang mate, grasped Storm's arm, his fingers biting into her flesh. Storm squealed with fright. People turned, looking worried. The tannoy system echoed throughout the station, distracting commuters with the announcement that the Tunbridge Wells train had been delayed by forty minutes. The plight of the distressed teenagers was momentarily forgotten.

"Get off me!" Storm screamed wriggling furiously.

Numerous concerned eyes met hers.

"Help me!" she shouted.

"Is everything alright?" A tall woman asked. She had blonde hair wound up into a bun, a lavish cream coat with matching shoes and handbag. Expensive perfume wafted from her.

"My daughter!" explained Welsh. "She has mental health issues and keeps running away."

The woman nodded but looked unconvinced.

"I'm not his daughter. He's a dirty Paedo. Paedophile!" Storm shrieked. "Call the Police!"

Spinning, she managed to kick Welsh in the shins. He shouted in pain. Turning her to face him, he shook her, slapping her face hard. Storm cried out in agony and distress as blood surged to her injured face.

"That's quite enough! I don't care who you are!" The blonde woman scolded Welsh, looking horrified.

"Mind your own business you ugly old hag!" Welsh snarled, shoving the woman violently, she, cried out and staggered backwards. Kicking out, Welsh's foot hit her stomach and she tumbled into a group of men wearing black wool coats. The blonde lady hit the shiny white station floor with a thud.

The station erupted into chaos. Fellow businesspeople surged forward to assist her. Several whipping out mobile phones, chattering frantically into them. Others were trying to take photos and video of Welsh's face and the scene. Welsh moved up his scarf covering his features.

Finn twisted and turned, wriggling out of Balaclavas' firm grip. Then he felt what Storm had seen. The muzzle of a cold hard pistol digging into his back.

"The bald dudes got a gun!" yelled Storm in desperation.

Screams and shouts of panic filled the station. Storm stamped violently on Welsh's foot repeatedly. He shrieked with anguish. Wrenching her arm away she turned, kneeing him in the groin. He cried in pain, a high-pitched sound!

Finn remembering a Kung Fu move he'd learnt years ago at school, grated Balaclava's shin with the heel of his boot. Balaclava yelled, loosening his grip, snarling, and swearing into Finn's ear. Pushing him away he turned Finn to face him, pointing the pistol to his chest. As he went to pull the trigger, Finn bashed Balaclava's under arm, upwards, just as the pistol fired. A loud gunshot echoed round the station. The bullet missed Finn by inches, embedding itself in the ceiling.

Screams resonated, as crowds of hysterical people ran in terror from the scene.

Storm leapt onto Balaclava's back, pressing pressure points located under his chin with her fingers. His neck was thick and solid, but it distracted him, and Finn managed to hit his wrist, knocking the pistol onto the floor. Storm jumped down kicking the pistol across the station out of reach. Finn punched Balaclava in the face.

"Just a mild punishment." he growled as Balaclava's nose erupted into a mass of scarlet.

The crowd surged towards the main entrance, trying to exit the station, colliding with confused, incoming commuters battling their way in.

"Run!" Shouted Finn.

Following the mass frenzy, they were carried along with the mob. Welsh, grabbed hold of Storm's hoody, pulling her backwards. She fell onto her back, on the floor. Boots and shoes trampled her body. Finn manically punched and kicked, his way back over to her. Grabbing Storm by her clothes, he pulled her bruised body upwards. The shrill sound of police whistles and authoritative voices boomed, ordering calm, telling the public to exit the station immediately in an orderly manner. Attempting to reach Welsh and Balaclava, Police searched the crowd frantically, looking for signs of Storm and Finn, after hearing reports from the assaulted blonde woman with the bun, of an attempted abduction of a young girl by a sex fiend.

Chattering echoed on radios as backup was requested for firearm officers and rapid response. The limited police presence in the station was inadequate to deal with the situation with only three officers to tackle both Welsh, Balaclava, hundreds of petrified commuters, and to hunt for two allusive teenagers. Outraged members of the public suffered bruises and fat lips, as they helped detain a very angry Balaclava and Welsh, who were throwing kicks and punches, shouting, and swearing in an effort to flee before the police arrested them.

With hoods up, Finn and Storm merged into the sea of bodies finally managing to reach the safety of the outside taxi rank. Lifting Storm up into his arms like a baby, Finn barged to the front of the queue shouting in a grown up, upper class English accent.

"My partner has fainted and is injured. She's pregnant. May I take the first taxi please, she needs urgent medical attention."

Without waiting for a response, they clambering into the first taxi. Finn helped Storm onto the slippery black leather seat.

"Finsbury Park Station please, as quick as you can." Finn slammed the door waving a fifty-pound note in the air.

The taxi screeched off at top speed.

"You alright?" Finn looked at Storm's pale bruised face. "Matching bruises! I can't stop shaking!"

"Just want to go home." Tears rolled down her face, her bottom lip trembling.

"How much money we got left?" Finn whispered as they pulled up to a traffic light.

"Had one K. Minus train fare down here and taxi, left about seven fifty, bikes we nicked two hundred, so five fifty, groceries fifty, phone and food another fifty. That's four fifty. Train one hundred, so three fifty left. But there's two hundred left in the tool belt. So, we have five hundred and fifty."

"Let's chance it. The police hopefully have arrested Welsh and Balaclava. Worse scenario we have a head start." Finn tapped on the glass. "How much to Peterborough mate?"

The taxi driver eyed Storm.

"Your misses, ok?"

"Pregnant and feeling bit shit." said Finn.

"Mrs Brown, me misses when she was preggers, 'ad sickness somefink awful. We got hitched young too. Still together."

Finn smiled and nodded.

"Where you 'eading?"

"Peterborough."

"Do it for a ton? Hundred."

Scrambling out at Peterborough. Finn paid and thanked the taxi driver.

"Cheers mate."

He helped Storm out of the taxi.

"Battered." said Storm as they bought tickets out of the machine for Alnwick in the North of England.

"You took a fair trampling." Finn smiled.

The train inched into the station.

"Thank God. Train's in." He added.

The red and grey train glided along the steel rails. Boarding, they took their seats. It was almost empty with just a smattering of passengers.

"We get off at Alnwick, taxi to North Shields, pay one of the Trawler Skippers a few hundred to drop us at Dunbar harbour." Said Finn. "So done with this need to get to safety. There's euros in the tool belt too. Can give them those too."

"Give them all the treasure! Just want to get back to Puffin Island!"

"Feel the same. Nightmare! Jez I can't even process it!"

Storm took his hand.

"If you hadn't bashed his arm upwards..." Tears welled up in her eyes.

"I know! I'd be dead! Mental as it sounds, I can't get my head around the fact that Balaclava tried to kill me! I mean, he actually pulled the trigger! How could anyone…in cold blood! I'm a kid… and for money! Bloody evil…"

"Revenge, not just money! Remember Finn, his brother was John the Psycho. It was beyond terrifying." She shook her head.

"Is your face ok?"

Storm's cheek boasted a red and purple bruise.

"I'll live. Well, I hope I will!"

"No wonder I had a bad feeling before heading down to camp." said Finn shaking his head. "What a few days. Feel sick to be honest. Not even hungry!"

"Now that is tragic. You must be totally traumatised!" Storm went to laugh but winced with discomfort as her ribs were bruised. "Hope that blonde lady's ok. If it hadn't been for her."

"Seemed ok." Finn nodded. "Welsh knocked her flying. Real nasty. Yeah, she played a major part in us getting away."

The trolley bumped and jangled down the aisle.

"Any refreshments or snacks?" The pretty dark hostess asked.

"Two large packets of peanuts, bottles of water and two hot chocolates please." Said Storm, paying for snacks.

Sipping hot chocolate, the heated sugary flavour of cocoa beans transported them to the Emerald Pool Chamber. Bashed, battered, and exhausted, Storm and Finn looked out of the window as flashes of green landscape zoomed past their eyes.

"Nearly there." Finn reassured.

"I really, really hope so." said Storm.

Rain began to fall throwing dashes of water onto the rectangle windows. Storm's eyes closed and she fell into a deep sleep. Finn sat watching her. Adrenaline pumped around his body. Every nerve was on high alert! A dark hatred sat in his chest towards

Balaclava, Welsh and the gang. He couldn't comprehend that someone was willing to take his life so causally. He was fifteen and hadn't even sat his end of school exams yet. The moment that pistol fired, Finn had grown up! His childhood and teenage years were over. He would protect Storm and himself at all costs for now and for the rest of their natural lives, of that he swore to himself.

Balaclavas smug face hovered in front of his eyes. Finn glared at the image. Hopefully he and his mate Welsh would be locked up in a cell by now, charged with assault and possession of an illegal firearm, to name but a few offences. There would be CCTV and witnesses to back up the charges. The gang had screwed up massively.

Finn decided that they would go out diving in the Firth of Forth as soon as possible. They could explore, swim, sit and talk things out. One thing Finn had learned from Storm was that talking helped release anger and pain and Finn certainly had enough of that to fill ten lifetimes. As they reached Newcastle, most of the passengers left the train. Only an elderly couple boarded. As the train pulled off, he felt his shoulders relax slightly. Even if they had to steal a boat, he would make sure they returned to Puffin Island by midnight. There was only so much two young people could take and they had reached their limit.

CHAPTER 17
A Shock and a Row

As the train approached Durham, Finn gently nudged Storm awake.

"Storm, wake up!"

Storm opened her eyes.

"Where are we?" she asked sleepily.

"Near Durham. Alnwick is past North Shields, not before as we thought."

"Really!"

"Yeah, Guard said."

"Could just stay on the train, or get another taxi?"

"Too risky. We don't know who's still about. Maybe Hippy Claire and her bald husband are on the prowl. It's more dangerous the nearer we get. I get it. I'm done too!"

Arriving at Durham Station, Finn and Storm left the train. While Storm went to the bathroom, Finn conducted a thorough visual search of the station and car park. There was no sign of Balaclava or his gang. A solitary white taxi sat outside. Finn approached the taxi driver

"North Shield's Fish Quay please." he said.

The taxi driver nodded and drove off. Storm and Finn glanced at each other. They were both so tense and suspicious of everyone. They dared not speak for fear they divulge information to the enemy. Silence reigned for most of the duration of the journey. Easy listening music from the radio filled the car.

Sunset had passed. The sky was a dark grey streaked with white and blue. The clock on the dashboard of the car read 7.30pm.

"Do you think anyone will be about at this time? said Finn

"Who knows." said Storm looking warily at the back of the driver's head.

Arriving at the harbour, they found it empty. Walking to the quayside they looked around in despair.

"God damn, we can't wait 'til morning!" cried Finn angrily. Rain began to fall. "Should have stayed on the train like you said. Idiot I am!"

"You kids alright?" A head popped out of the cabin of a small fishing trawler.

It was a man of about seventy years of age. He had brown weathered skin, twinkly light blue eyes, and a long white beard. Dressed in grey overalls he looked fit and muscular.

"Need to get to Dunbar by sea?" Blurted out Storm. "It's like urgent. We can pay!"

The fisherman lit a cigarette.

"Why sea? Why not get a bus or train?"

Finn and Storm exchanged glances.

"Not runaways, are you?"

"Trying to get home, that's the problem." Storm burst into tears of frustration.

"Now now!. Don't be upsetting yourself. You stay Dunbar."

"Kinda near it. We can't say, but we can pay £300," said Finn.

The fisherman looked up at the sky and then at the bedraggled pair.

"Don't quite understand but the money'll certainly come in

handy."

"That a yes?"

"Aye a yes." The Fisherman helped Storm and Finn on to the boat, taking in their bruised faces.

"Looks like you two 'ave been in the wars. Names James by the way."

"You've no idea." replied Storm. "I'm Poppy and this is Charlie."

The ocean was black, as they motored slowly out of the harbour entrance into the vast North Sea. The moon shone down lighting a pathway. A light breeze replaced the rain, and the sky was clear and full of bright silver stars. Trillions of souls watched their progress as they journeyed up the coast to Dunbar.

The Fisherman told them tales as they travelled.

"An' the story is that treasure was lost at sea between Burntisland and Shelly many moons ago. Worth a fortune and never found!" He ended dramatically.

Finn and Storm glanced at each other and started laughing.

"It's no joke. It's a true tale." James said indignantly.

"No, no we believe you. Just a happy tale." explained Finn, trying to cover their reaction.

"Right you are." The fisherman took a swig of whisky from his hip flask." Be there soon and I might as well go out for the morning catch. You is good for the money like?"

Finn took out the three hundred and added another fifty.

"You saved us. You have no clue. The extra's for the fuel."

James the fisherman looked pleased.

"Been a fine day's work! Be able to buy me wife this necklace she's wanted for years." He nodded. "Been a fine day alright."

Dropping them at the harbour edge. The Fisherman waved and motored back out to sea.

"Nice old dude." said Finn following Storm along the quayside.

"Feels nice that he's got money to buy his wife a present. All good deeds and all that."

Storm pointed excitedly to the motorboat still parked where she had left it.

"Oh, thank God!" exclaimed Finn.

They jumped aboard the boat and Storm quickly whipped out her keys and started the engine.

"Homeward bound! I can't believe it!"

"What if the enemy's still at the Light House?" pondered Finn.

"We'll tell her the police are on their way. They know what they've done. Hippy Claire will run for sure. Hope the cats are ok!"

"You left the window open right!"

"Yeah."

Bouncing over the midnight waves, they could see the lamp at the top of the Lighthouse Tower flashing in the distance. Storm squealed with excitement.

"Jez my ear drum!" muttered Finn.

"Oh my God, Puffin Island!" Storm shouted over the roar of the motor as the island appeared. Sea spray cast up into the air and soaked their faces. But neither of them cared. They were nearly home.

The lights were on in the house and approaching Puffin Island Quay they saw a black speed boat they didn't recognise.

"Who do you think that belongs to?" Storm said nervously cutting the engine.

Clambering out of the boat they stood on the quayside, while Storm secured the boat.

"Where the hell have you two been?" A deep voice boomed.

In the doorway of the Light House stood a tall man with dark skin and hair. Dressed in jeans, a t-shirt and trainers. His face was full of anger.

"Dad!" whispered Finn taking a step back.

The shock of seeing his father alive and visible for the first time in over a year was too much for Finn after the ordeal he'd just been through. Storm placed a reassuring hand in the small of his back.

"We've been worried sick! Search parties are out!" Josh shouted.

Lily appeared at the door.

"Oh, thank God." Running down to the quay she hugged Storm and then Finn. "Your faces! Josh help them in."

"Nice to see you too Dad." Said Finn sourly, glaring at his father as he approached him.

"Everyone come sit in the lounge. The fires on." insisted Lily. "They look awful!" she added to Josh.

Josh nodded closing the front door after them.

"You two sit and get warm. I'll make us all a drink. Then we can talk. Josh, you come and help."

He followed Lily obediently.

"You ok Finn?" Storm whispered.

"No. Not quite the reunion I'd hoped for. But then nothing ever turns out as it's supposed to." He said angrily.

"They're just worried."

"Like I haven't been the last year."

"They obviously have no clue what happened."

"No clue about what?" asked Lily returning with steaming mugs of hot chocolate, chicken and ham sandwiches and crisps.

"We'll start the explanation." said Storm. "I don't think you realise what's gone on. Did you think we'd run away? Storm took a sip of hot chocolate. It was delicious.

Lily poured herself a glass of red wine. The fire crackled merrily in the grate. The orange and purple flames ignorant of the strained atmosphere in the room.

"Didn't know what to think." Lily said. "Came back early from the trip after I phoned the camp and they said you and Finn had decided to leave as you didn't like it there. Gone to Wales with friends you'd met there. That's all they knew. Your Dad was frantic as his intel backed it up."

"His intel?"

"One of his team. Alun Jones, Special Forces, was given the task to keep an eye on you both to make sure nothing happened whilst you were at adventure camp. It was supposed to be a safe place while we were all away."

Storm and Finn looked at each other.

"Welsh!" They said in unison.

"Yes, he is Welsh. He disappeared from adventure camp, then showed up in London earlier today." She glanced at her watch. "Yesterday now. Apparently arrested at Waterloo along with Harry Stanley who also used to be in Special Forces but left a few years back. Apparently, he's a suspected paedophile! Your Dad's going mental! He and Grandad Flint went down to the camp, then headed off to Wales. You two seemed to have disappeared off the face of the earth. I came home in case you turned up, and the house was deserted, and freezing! Window open, angry cats and the hallway littered with dead mice."

"We now know Alun Jones or Welsh, has gone rogue." said Josh. "You've grown son." He said to Finn. "Was worried sick. I didn't mean to shout."

"He has gone rogue." confirmed Finn. He ignored his Father's apology. Anger bubbled within him. "Storm do you want to start." He added gently.

"Hang on." Lily facetimed Storm's Dad. "They're safe and well Flint...yes they're going to say what happened now. Is Pops there with you? Good." She smiled at Storm. "Go ahead."

"I couldn't face it. Camp. I emailed and cancelled my booking from your laptop Mum when you were in the bath." Storm said quietly. "Gave a false email for any response. Headed back here and camped out in one of the caves. Then discovered Hippy Claire your friend and her bald husband were in league with the counterfeit gang who had the yacht out in the bay."

Josh nodded.

"We had suspicions, aye Flint."

"Yup Josh, we did. Carry on Storm." Storm's Dad said.

"Finn went to camp. We said we'd keep in touch no matter what. We texted as promised and then nothing from Finn! I knew something was wrong so went down there."

"Why didn't you call me?" Lily said in frustration.

"Should have but was only sure things were bad when I got there. Tried to call from camp but no signal. Then my phone was damaged. It fell out of a tree!"

"Oh God." Lily covered her face with her hand.

Finn continued the tale.

"When I got there, I was paired with this creepy dude called Adrian. Turns out he was older and is Jane, Hippy Claire's sister's son. They, along with Adrian's stepdad, were in the pay of the gang. Whilst out on a kayaking lesson they grabbed me, put some stuff over my nose and mouth that smelt rank."

"Is that what happened to your face." Josh's expression was one of silent rage.

"Yeah, well that happened later. Woke in this dark room. They were furious 'cos Storm wasn't there. They'd planned to kidnap us both to get the money back you took, and then kill us! They made that clear."

144

"I'm sorry son." Josh rubbed his hand over his short hair.

"You should be!" Finn sprang to his feet. "That's the second time I've nearly got killed 'cos of your stupid bloody job!" He shouted.

"We had things in place..." Josh tried to explain.

"We'll your obviously not that good at your job are you!" Finn walked towards his father. "If it hadn't been for Storm, I would be dead now! Where the hell were you?"

"He's been through a lot." said Storm to her uncle.

Finn stood glaring at his father. He was taller than him but not as muscular.

"You need to calm down Finn." Josh said. "I'll explain."

Finn wasn't listening. A year of fear, grief and worry erupted.

"And you have the bloody cheek to have a go at me for going AWOL when you just vanished without a word. Any idea how I felt. Stuck down in Gravestone with John the Psycho and Mum being torn apart, then finding out he was gonna kill us! Everyone thought you were dead but me! Then suddenly it turns out you're alive but didn't put your son out of his misery by telling him! Sneaking around hiding in the locked room like some ...some..."

Finn couldn't find the words.

"And you too Dad!" Storm angrily joined in. "You're just as bad! Finn was nearly shot! Could you be more selfish, both of you!"

Josh looked from one to the other.

"We thought we had things in place." Josh snapped at Storm. "It wasn't intentional to put you in danger." Fear laced his words with aggression.

"Don't you ever speak to her like that! She saved my life and is always there for me! She's worth ten of you!" roared Finn, squaring up to his father.

"Finn. Sit down." Said Lily calmly. "Please. Everyone's clearly upset."

Finn slumped back down on the sofa.

"Sorry Aunty. Just a bit stressed."

Storm put her hand on his arm.

"We should have known. Yes, we let you down." Storm's Dad's voice came from the phone. "So, so sorry. Storm. Can you carry on with the account?"

"Before I dropped my phone, I'd located Finn through 'locations' and seen his emoji on Fenton Isle. Took a boat over there and managed to unlock the screw hinges of the door where they'd imprisoned him and got him out." She continued.

"Storm brought the diving kit with the small air cannisters, and we swam underwater to Arne this nature place and made our way 'cross the fields to this old mansion. The gang turned up there, but we sneaked away unseen and nicked a couple of bikes and made it to the station. My phone had been smashed by this stocky Dude we called Balaclava."

"Stanley!" said Josh. "Apologies Storm, I didn't mean to snap."

"It's ok Uncle Josh. When we arrived at Waterloo it was packed. Balaclava or Stanley or whatever, had a pistol. Welsh grabbed me and smacked me in the face." said Storm.

Lily winced.

"This blonde woman intervened, and he knocked her flying. Station was full of businesspeople, and they called the police. Balaclava pointed a gun at Finn's chest." Her voice began to shake, and tears rolled down her face. "Finn bashed his arm upwards just as he pulled the trigger. He was nearly shot dead Uncle Josh. It's why he's so upset."

The adults looked at each other in horror, even Storm's Dad was quiet on the other end of the phone.

Josh strode across the room and took Finn into his arms cradling him.

"I'm so, so sorry son. I swear I will never let you down again." He said. "Or you Storm."

"Likewise, Storm and you too Finn." Storm's Dad's voice sounded gutted. "Jez had no idea. This is bad."

Josh sat down next to Finn on the sofa.

"You know first-hand how evil this gang are. We had made masses of preparations at the camp to protect you both. Jones or Welsh as you call him, wrecked all of them and did the opposite by kidnapping you Finn and feeding us false information. The gang are responsible for destroying thousands of lives through drugs, slavery, people trafficking. It's why I had to go undercover and then hide. The work was that important."

"We need to be better than this, and we're so sorry." Flint said sincerely through the video link. "You managed to escape from Waterloo." He prompted.

"Yeah, we got a taxi to Peterborough. Train to Durham. Taxi to North Shields, then paid a Fisherman to take us to Dunbar. Just trying to stay off the radar!"

Josh nodded his approval.

"You two put us to shame. Right Flint."

"Proud of you both." said Flint.

"For sure." said Josh.

"Took the motorboat I 'd left at Dunbar and headed back. And here we are." Finished Storm.

"Thank God!" Lily poured a large glass of wine with a shaking hand. "Too young to have to deal with all this!"

"You both ok?" Grandad Flint's voice came over the phone. He was clearly thinking the same thing.

"Yeah Pops." Storm and Finn said.

"Gang's gone to ground after the arrest of Stanley and Jones. We'll hunt them out and not rest 'til we capture each and every last one of them." Grandad Flint continued.

"We good son?" Josh looked Finn in the eye.

Finn nodded.

"Storm's got bruised ribs and prob needs to rest up."

"Right bed for you two." announced Lily. "Can catch up properly tomorrow."

They said goodnight. Storm and Finn made their way up to the Zen room. Storm looked in at her bedroom on the way. It was round and perfect as she had left it. There'd been quite a few times she thought she'd never see it again.

Lighting the wood burner and lemon scented candles, Storm made a bed out of large soft cushions and laid down next to Finn who was on the sofa.

"Not quite ready to be alone yet." said Storm covering herself with the thick red fleecy blanket.

"Same. Glad you're close by." Finn snuggled down under his duvet.

"Can't believe we made it back. We are actually here, aren't we?"

"We are. Tomorrow we'll have hot chocolate and chips by the fire like we said, looking out across the waves. And when your ribs are ok, we'll go treasure hunting in the Firth." Said Finn.

"Great idea. We'll be ok." whispered Storm. "Why am I whispering?"

Marmite walked in and jumped on the sofa next to Finn and curled up contently. Marmalade appeared moments later sneaking furtive glances at his brother. Furiously washing herself she butted Storm and lay down in the curve of her belly.

"Can't believe my dad's here. It's like surreal. Like a weird dream. Dunno what Mum'll think when she's home."

"Totally. Maybe they'll talk things out."

"Night night Storm. We're home on Puffin Island!"

"I know! Thank God. Night night Finn."

CHAPTER 18

The Emerald Pool Chamber and a Discovery

Storm climbed the curved icy marble staircase. Reaching the landing, a sudden warmth nursed her frozen bare feet as they sank into the lush thick cream carpet covering the floor. Wandering along the hallway, she climbed steps that led to the left turreted room of the Dorset mansion. The round room was bathed in the first light of dawn. She stood gazing through small, panelled lead light windows, across green meadows dotted with orange, yellow and burgundy forests. The sea gleamed, a strip of inky black in the distance. An indigo glow covered the sky. Storm could see Puffin Island in the distance with its lamp flashing out pulses of red. Red for danger! SOS!

Storm awoke with a start, sweat clinging to her body. Kicking off the thick blanket, she frantically took in her surroundings. Relief and reassurance comforted her. For a mere moment upon waking, she thought she was back in the mansion in Dorset. A glow of heat flickered, drifting from the small amber flames in the wood burner, curling around radiant ruby embers coated in charcoal.

Finn jerked, turning in his sleep. The movement propelled Marmite from his warm spot next to Finn and he landed with a plop onto Storm's bed. Marmite looked cross and began washing himself, before stalking out of the door to the kitchen, hissing at his brother Marmalade as he went.

Storm climbed out of the snug camp bed and put another log onto the fire. It hissed and popped with greedy pleasure devouring the offering. The room felt warm and safe, and Storm stood looking out of the vast windows at the heaving gun metal grey ocean. The sky was a light grey and the wind tugged at the branches of the trees in the bottle green forest below.

The journey, rescue and escape had seemed endless, as if time had frozen or slowed down. No matter what they'd done to stay off the radar, Balaclava and his men had caught up with them. Storm couldn't quite believe it was all over. School aside, being hunted was the worse feeling she'd ever experienced. Constantly on high alert, suspicious, paranoid, and scared, plus being so physically active, was draining. Recovery would take time, but Storm agreed with Finn, treasure hunting and exploration of the Firth of Forth, was the excellent distraction they both needed.

Her ribs were bruised but already less sore. They'd make a picnic and return to the underworld of Puffin Island. The safest place on the planet, where no one could find them!

Finn muttered in his sleep, his face was healing, and the bruises had turned a brownish yellow around his cheekbone. Storm went down to the kitchen to feed the cats. They meowed and butted her with gratitude, happy that Hippy Claire was no longer there.

Her round bathroom called to her. Filling the bath with hot lemon scented water, Storm soaked her bruised body, then washed her filthy hair. She'd been too tired the night before and her mother hadn't pressed it.

"Storm you about?" Finn's deep booming voice called down the stairs.

"In the bath!" She yelled wincing, as her ribs were still tender.

"Dying for the loo!"

"Use the downstairs!"

She could hear him padding down the stairs in bare feet and the door to the Lighthouse Tower opening and closing.

After drying, she dressed in black yoga pants, trainers, a white t-shirt, and black hoody, winding her long dark green hair up into a bun on the top of her head.

Cleaning her teeth, she glanced down at the red bucket by the sink. The long lump of coral they'd discovered in the Ghost Ship before the calamity at adventure camp, was submerged in water and washing up liquid. The hard, coral that clung to the object had partially fallen away leaving patches of silver shining through.

The door banged and the musky smell of male deodorant wafted up the staircase ahead of Finn, who'd showered and dressed in a black tracksuit, t-shirt, and trainers.

"Finn." Storm shouted from the bathroom, replacing her toothbrush.

"Err...you decent?"

"Don't be gross. Yeah, I'm dressed. Come look at this!" She called.

Finn poked his head in the door, feigning relief as he saw her fully clothed.

"It's been soaking in there a week."

Finn crouched down by the bucket.

"What is it do you think? See bits of metal. A spoon. Oh my God!"

"What?"

"Charles 1st missing serving spoon." He said in an upper-class English accent.

"Not that one again. You're like obsessed!"

He rubbed more coral from the long shape.

"Hard to know what's coral and what's whatever it is, the metal thing. Coral's kinda gone like old clay now, flaky but sticky from soaking in that liquid. Look Storm, it's falling away. Pass us that cloth thing....no the weird green thing with the sponge."

"You mean the sponge that cleans the bathroom. Know why you have no clue what that is." Storm smiled, handing her cousin the sponge. She crouched next to him.

Years of entombment fell away from the mysterious object.

The smell of bacon, sausages, waffles, and eggs drifted up from the kitchen.

"Oh, Aunt Lilly said breakfasts in five mins. Feel like I've been starved a thousand years."

"Slight exaggeration Finn, you stuffed most of the chicken sandwiches last night!"

"That gangster dude nearly starved me to death. Still haven't caught up."

Storm laughed.

"Let me have a go."

Rubbing gently, a large lump of clag fell to the bottom of the bucket. Storm gasped with excitement and Finn's eyes gleamed.

"It's what I thought!" he said with excitement.

"Pass that white flannel, cloth thing and the bubble bath."

Lathering the flannel with soap she cleaned the remainder of the coral from the deep dark waters of the Creepy Cave, and held up a tarnished sliver object.

"You thought it was Charles 1 serving spoon."

"Well yeah kinda, but who wants some old spoon when...." He took it from Storm holding it up. "You can have an ancient dagger!" Finn squinted at the engraving down the handle. "It's still a bit rusty and tarnished but it's intact."

"Can get some special stuff to remove rust and other crap."

Finn nodded excitedly. They cleaned out the bucket and placed the dagger back in hot soapy water.

"Looks like some kinda symbols on the handle."

The handle of the dagger was about three inches long, and one inch thick boasting Celtic symbols, covered in grime.

Aunt Lilly's voice called for the second time.

"Breakfast!"

The blade was about four inches graduating into a jagged point.

"There's some kinda writing down the blade."

"Careful. It's still a lethal weapon. Leave it in the bucket longer. There's a bunch of cleaning stuff for brass and silver under the sink. We can use that."

Storm and Finn headed to the dining room, where they were greeted by Josh and Lily. The bay stretched out for miles through the picture windows. The sea rolled large waves of navy blue. Plump fluffy clouds drifted across the baby blue sky. The purple and orange fire crackled in the grate of the log burner.

"It's so weird seeing you sitting there Dad." said Finn forking waffle, bacon, sausage, and egg. "Like good. But just weird."

"How can you fit all that in your mouth?" Storm exclaimed at his piled fork.

"Easily." said Finn and groaned with pleasure as he shovelled it into his mouth.

Josh and Lily laughed.

"It's good to be here Finn." said Josh. "Your Mum's doing ok by the way. Haven't told her what happened with you guys, as she's still in treatment at the clinic, but the Doctor's told her I'm alive." He grinned. "Hopefully that won't set her back."

"Hmmm yeah…always a danger." Finn's eyes twinkled.

"See you two are back to normal already!" laughed Lily.

"What about Dad and Grandad Flint?" asked Storm.

"Back tonight." said Josh. "Police'll want to take a statement over next couple of days. Nothing to worry about. Just tell them what happened after you left Puffin Island Finn." He took a sip of tea. "And Storm just the bit about you not wanting to go to adventure camp and returning to Puffin Island. Tell them you camped out in the Cave on the west beach, but after not hearing from Finn you were worried and headed to Poole. The rest of what happened after that you can say. They don't need to know about overhearing Claire and her husband talking. That'll keep certain things safe."

Finn and Storm nodded in agreement. Their orders were clear. Under no circumstances were they to divulge the secrets of Puffin Island to anyone ever.

"Do know about Jane, Instructor Tom and the weird dude Adrian?" asked Finn. "You not eating that sausage." He eyed the sausage pushed to the side on Storm's plate.

"Have it!"

"Yeah. Just trying to locate them and get Welsh Jones and Balaclava Stanley to spill their guts about the rest of the gang, specially the ringleader. They're saying nothing so far which is expected, but annoying. They'll crack!"

"What's the plan today?" asked Storm's mother.

"Gonna chill and explore. We were wondering if we could have tea in the Zen room later. We kinda had a fantasy about chips, salt and tomato sauce along with hot chocolate when we were on the run." Said Finn.

"Sure." Josh smiled. "Plenty of time to catch up Finn as I'm back for a bit."

"That's cool." Finn nodded.

"Be careful!" said Lily. "Enough excitement for one year!"

"Second that." said Josh.

"What are you guys up to?" asked Storm.

"Putting Uncle Josh to work converting the outhouses into living quarters." Lily smiled. "I'm starting a new batch of paintings."

"Oh, how did the exhibition go?" asked Storm.

"Good. Got a few commissions," Lily smiled. Art and painting were her true passion in life, and it meant a lot to her, to be recognised as a serious artist.

Standing in the kitchen Storm and Finn prepared a pack lunch of cheese sandwiches, tomato soup, pasties, and hot chocolate.

Storm turned to Finn. Smiling with pure excitement she squeezed his arm.

"Can't wait. So excited!"

"I know!" Finn said. "Will truly feel I'm back and safe when I'm swimming in the waters of the Emerald Pool Chamber." He patted the black rucksack. "Fill the cannisters and off we go. Sure, you're up to it."

"You managed it after nearly drowning that time. So, I can too." Storm said firmly.

"We're different aren't we, than we were a few months back." said Finn suddenly. "Kinda grown up now."

"How could we not be, after all that!" Storm agreed as they made their way down into the lower cellar.

Taking the keys from the Keeper of Keys, Storm clicked open the entrance to the tunnel and the underworld of Puffin Island. They made their way down the cold iron rungs embedded into the walls. Storm clicked the large torch beam on as Finn closed over the trap door. The beam happily bobbed once more along the zigzagging passageway, and they felt tension oozing out of their bodies at the sight of the secure and familiar surroundings.

Storm opened the door to the Emerald Pool Chamber while Finn sorted out the diving kit. They lit the candles and lanterns. The cool emerald, green water glittered magically. Storm unpacked the lunch, placing it onto the shelf that ran around the chamber.

Taking out blankets and towels, she changed into her wet suit and laid Finn's out for him.

Finn returned with the diving gear.

"Reckon we'll just have a swim around the Ghost Ship, Coded Archways and a small bit of the Forth, not too far out." said Finn getting changed.

"Agreed. Have plenty of time for other stuff."

Plunging into the cold water, they pulled down their goggles, inserted mouth pieces and flicked air switches to ON. Swimming through the Arch, passing Dome of Breath 1, they squeezed by the fallen boulder and out into the deep dark waters of the Creepy Cave. The Ghost Ship stared at them out of coral encrusted eyes. Finn and Storm felt a fondness for the ship. They too had undergone distress and trauma, like the wrecked vessel and understood what it was to feel true fear, and near peril.

Swimming around the starboard side, they made their way through swaying long lime sea grass, a jungle of brown clumped seaweed dotted with strange yellow and burgundy plants and vast brown boulders, to the Coded Archways.

Hovering, Storm punched into the panel the code for TREASURE. The synthetic door clunked, swinging open. Swimming through into the Dome of Breath 2, Storm and Finn exchanged glances remembering when they had first discovered the codes and finally after much pondering and searching, the secret hiding place of the Key to the Locked Room. Finn punched in the code for ISLAND, and they swam through the second manmade door, closing it securely behind them, before entering the Sea Well and floating upwards into the underwater rock pool.

Surfacing they arrived back on the surface of Puffin Island. Seagulls chattered loudly, their shrill shrieks filling the air. The day was still bright and sunny with a clear cobalt blue sky and glinting indigo ocean. The air was laced with an overpowering scent of salt, and fishy seaweed. Storm and Finn clambered over the dividing wall of the rock pool, lowering into the deep mysterious waters of the Firth of Forth. Duck diving down, they swam through sea water. The water was clean and clear. Small fish and numerous crabs stared at them inquisitively. The sandy seabed was littered with seashells, old pieces of orange fishing nets, rocks, and odd items. Storm pointed to an old boot lying forlornly on the bottom. An old engine, possibly from the wreck of a motorboat lay next to it.

Finn suddenly stopped swimming, grabbing Storm as a warning. A large shape loomed ahead. A humming noise came from it. Flashing the beam, all they could see was a wall of grey. Storm was terrified! Finn turned and pointed back the way they'd come. Storm rapidly blew air bubbles in panic. Following Finn, they resurfaced near the underwater rockpool, and swam back to the barrier.

"What the hell?" began Storm.

"Let's get back." Finn scrambled over the barrier wall almost falling headfirst into the Sea Well in his haste.

Storm tuning into his fear, followed suit and dived downwards. Punching in the code ISLAND they entered Dome of Breath 2. Finn pulled the door shut behind them, double checking that that it was locked. He then checked the panel to the Key. Happy that was secure, Storm punched in the code TREASURE, and they re-entered the Creepy Cave, making sure again the door had locked behind them.

At speed they swam back to the Emerald Pool Chamber and climbed out of the water.

Taking off their kit, they changed into warm dry clothes.

"What the hell Finn." said Storm her teeth chattering as she towel dried her hair. "Was it a whale or what? Totally, totally freaked me out."

"Think it was a sub, like a surveillance submarine type thing."

"A sub." Storm laid out the blanket and they sat down. Covering their legs with a thicker brown fleece cover, she poured steaming hot chocolate into mugs. "Where did you get that from? Was big and grey, could have been a whale.... too cold for sharks though, right?

"Humming? A quiet engine? Unless it was a mechanical whale..." Finn pulled a face and scratched his head.

They burst out laughing. They laughed and laughed until tears streamed down Storm's cheeks.

"Ouch my ribs. Ours? Please say that subs ours! Not theirs...that stupid gang...so, so done with them!"

"No clue. Say ours. Could have been passing. Bit close to the rocks, but they have navigation systems." said Finn confidently. "Too soon for that lot to regroup. Lost a heap of men, again!"

"Like you're now an expert on submarines." Storm laughed. "Feels good to laugh again. It's being here. Love it! Feel so happy."

"This hot chocolate is epic!" Finn drained his, pouring out tomato soup. "Seen it in a war film about this sub that navigates through enemy waters. Was cool and super interesting."

Finn and Storm dipped cheese sandwiches into tomato soup. It really was a delicious combination!

"Be happy days when that dude Tom and his little shit of a stepson Adrian, "call me Aidie" get busted and end up in the nick." nodded Finn.

"They'll get them. Special Forces are the best of the best." Storm agreed.

"So, love being back here. Dreamt of this place when I was kidnapped! Kept me going. You, me, and all this." said Finn. "But! How could I forget how cold it gets! Feet are actual ice blocks!"

They tidied away the kit and made their way back up to the lower cellar. Locking the entrance. The Keeper of Keys protected the keys to the underworld once more.

A note left on the kitchen breakfast bar read:

"Headmistress is coming for a routine progress check two weeks Monday. Nothing to worry about as all good and Pop's has your work and been keeping records. Gone to the Fort shopping. Be back later. Love you both. Xxx Mum/Aunty Lily. PS Josh/Dad has come too."

Heading up to the Zen room, Storm lit candles and the log burner. They sat on bean bags enjoying the warmth. Storm fetched the silver cleaner and gently cleaned the ancient weapon with the cleaner and a cotton wool pad.

Marmite was asleep on Finn's bed and Marmalade curled up in a fluffy ginger ball in front of the dancing cheerful orange flames of the fire. Rain began to lash against the windowpanes.

"Look Finn can just make it out. Lettering on the blade."

Finn disappeared and could be heard rummaging through one of the drawers in the hallway. He reappeared with a magnifying glass. Peering, they tried to make out the deep grooved lettering.

"Looks like Gaelic." said Storm. "Learnt some when I was up last in Shetland."

"Teàrlach E Stiùbhart 111." Storm read out. "Type it into the translate app Finn, quick!"

Finn stared at the results with his mouth open.

"Like you could look more gormless! What?" Storm demanded. "What Finn?"

He cleared his throat and announced dramatically:

"You are holding the dagger of Charles Edward Stuart 111, aka Bonnie Prince Charlie!"

Storm looked aghast.

"What! Oh my God, no way!"

"Hang on. I'll look it up." Finn typed into his phone "Seems he was about in 1745, like in Scotland before he fled, or something. No clue how the dagger ended up stuck in the wall of the Ghost Ship in our basement." He grinned. "But one thing is for sure…"

"What?" Storm was staring at the dagger incredulously.

Royalty had held the weapon that now lay on her lap. It was of massive historic value and would be worth a fortune.

"Our knowledge of history is terrible! All these Prince Charles's are majorly confusing! The lost treasure of Burntisland belonged to Charles 1. This is from Charles 111."

"They're awful careless with their stuff, these royals!" commented Storm.

"See what we've learnt. Every day's a school day." Said Finn nastily, grinned wickedly at Storm.

"Oh, shut up Finn." Storm knelt pummelling Finn over the head with a green cushion. "And yeah, still too soon to joke about it."

Marmalade looked up in annoyance at the commotion. Glanced at the fire and went back to sleep.

"Time for chips yet." said Finn roaring with laughter, dodging out of the way of Storm.

Laughter filled the rounded walls of the Lighthouse Tower. Finn and Storm were warm and safe once more. Outside, in the hidden deep dark depths of the ocean, a strange vessel moved silently and undetected, monitoring, gathering information and storing data. For now, all was peaceful on Puffin Island. However, it was, merely, the quiet before the arrival of the storm of storms!

THE END

Coming soon....:

Storm Swift
SOS Puffin Island

ABOUT THE AUTHOR

Stephanie De Winter

The author lives in East Lothian with her two children and two cats. She has been writing since an early age and the Storm Swift adventure series is inspired by the beautiful island of Fidra located in the Firth of Forth in Scotland.

PRAISE FOR AUTHOR

My daughter says it's her favourite book!

"My daughter loved reading this book. She was really inspired by the main characters which she said were very brave. She loved how adventurous the story was!"

Difficult to put down:

As an avid reader of the Famous Five books, I liked the fact that the story is set on an island with hidden tunnels and caves. The central character is likeable and relevant and the dialogue is entertaining and assumes an intelligent reader. I was captivated by the story as it picks up pace and is exciting. I look forward to the next book!

- A SMALL SELECTION OF REVIEWS

BOOKS BY THIS AUTHOR

Storm Swift And The Seventh Key

Puffin Island is home to Storm Swift. Her dark anxious world is transformed after she is suspended from school. From Hell School to Home School, Storm flourishes. Finn her cousin arrives on the island one stormy night after running away from his psychopathic step dad and together they discover the mysterious underworld of the island that contains tunnels, secrets, puzzles to be solved and a shipwreck.

Printed in Great Britain
by Amazon